I0533730

THE First ENVISAGE: rainstorm.

...the beginning...

By: Pluie D'amour (Rebecca Sue Spooner)

2013 ©Rebecca Sue Spooner. All Rights Reserved.

Pluie D'amour

Printed by CreateSpace

0615852386

First Edition

This novel is a work of fiction. Characters and circumstances (including Ms. Joslin O. Tilda) are mental property of the author, and any relation to living persons is purely circumstantial.

2013 © Rebecca Sue Spooner (Pluie D'amour)

978-0615852386

INTRODUCTION:

I always wonder about the past. The thoughts that recur in my head dilute my reality and make me feel as though I'm centuries old.

My differences aren't *too* alien, and I've had an average life (for the way circumstances were) yet *still* I create my delusions and succumb to them. They seem to save me and keep my parents near.

My parents are dead.

They die again and again in my head, because if people live in your thoughts, they can never really die for good. It doesn't make sense and puts me to sorrow.

So I dance when I'm allowed to dance. This makes me smile and think of their lives and how much they gave and had to give.

Dance brings life, because dance goes against the grain. It is natural movement, but more; it is art. Of course, art doesn't die; no matter how many times people may try to kill it.

I dance in pure and bare natures, in solitude and in the open. I dance because my body is many bodies, and they all desire movement. They all urge to be put in a sort of composure, the feet, the knees, the toes.

Each limb is a body and should be able to move if it so chooses, in the precise way it wills... isn't that the way that we're built?

Us humans?

Anyway, I've created a memory aside and apart from physical motion... I've created a telling of me. Hopefully, by describing what happened in reality, I'll find out what I'm supposed to be.

~Joslin O. Tilda

This first book of the "Envisage" series as written by Pluie D'amour (Rebecca Sue Spooner) is wholly dedicated to Mrs. Barbara Hazard for character and storyline inspiration.

Also thanks go to Katilyn Marie Davenport for her inspiration.

Special thanks go to my brilliant sister, Tiffany Spooner for her time, and dedicated work in the final edit. Also, thanks go to Christopher Watson for the initial thoughtful editing and Ty Kinsey for thoughtful critique and pleasant coffee time.

Other thanks go to family for their enormous support and friends who have been waiting for this book.

Again, all characters and scenarios in this novel are a fictional property of the author. Resemblances to real life are purely coincidental. All Rights Reserved.

Prior to reading this chapter... just read the small introduction, if you please.

Chapter 1: A Fantasy

"Aina, my love, my love, my LOVE!"

"What is..."

My mouth was halted with a pair of lips that painfully and lusciously abraded mine.

"Talib!" I exclaimed when our kiss broke, "What in God's name is wrong with..."

Again I stopped speaking. My wizard of a man gripped me tightly and I held onto him.

Now, I could share all of these details of our love-making, but what is private should be kept private. We two were amorous for each other and each other alone.

My—Our life started long ago in a forgotten age, and most of our stories will be read someday, I'm sure.

For now though I must only share essential information so that I can make clear records of my love, my child, Joslin O. Tilda.

She was conceived that night, long ago in the forgotten age. Talib had just returned from one of his journeys to a foreign land called "Husrodolg".

...The time period that we lived in was strange. It was an age of over one-hundred years that should have been (mostly) called "the seventh century".

However, historians never recorded any occurrences from the age, because life within the time-frame was estranged. Documentations and histories had all been deleted from the physical and mental world. Hence, I call it "forgotten".

"Aina-the-Ray": yes—that's me. I cannot tell you my birthdate. I really cannot tell you... It technically doesn't exist.

But *Talib* was born long before I was—born curious, covertly trying to discover new life and new worlds at every moment of every day.

Joslin was born in our bedroom one-thousand-four-hundred and eighty-five years after that romantic day (her conception) in a year that I *believe* should have been marked as 652a.d. However, she was not born as a human.

She transformed into a beautiful little girl over the next few days, but started life as a collection of faerie spirits called tharpels—

I can't tell you what tharpels look like,

because I, myself, can't see them. Talib has told me that they are slightly smaller than a human immunity cell, and they glow with a light similar to that of the moon, but I don't know what each separate entity looks like. Only one who has been to their homeland, "Husrodolg", is permitted to see them.

Mid-afternoon–January 23rd, 2137.

"Aina!" Talib shouted at me.

"What?!" I shouted back at him, startled.

I stared at him saying, "What?" repeatedly, while stressing about his utterly befuddled concentration on me.

"Just... don't shut your eyes..."

And I could *feel* the pressure. What seemed longer than 30 seconds of staring straight ahead was really about 5, and then he finally said, "Alright, you can blink," as he laughed at me.

Talib wasn't much of a trickster. I mean— sure he'd make fun of me constantly because I was crazy klutzy, but he didn't prank... at least not that I knew of.

"What in the *world?*" I asked him.

"I'll tell you in a moment, love," he said, marveling at his arms.

He kept looking at them, and I sat still—perplexed. I looked at his face with my eyebrows raised momentarily. Whereas, I would sometimes marvel—or gawk—at his arms, I'm his wife, and that's normal. He's an attractive man.

Talib was strange, but he always had a reason for things. He looked longingly at his own arms, which were crossed along his chest. I felt weird looking at him, but my confusion made me stare, my mind longing to settle the matter.

Growing antsy and irritable, I began switching my glances back and forth from him to my project of sorting through our pictures and paintings again.

Just a month ago, during December, we moved to this nice remote location in a rural Iowan area. For ten years we'd been in Iowa; we set ourselves up by suburbia. We surrounded ourselves with neighbors and people. There were plenty of parks nearby and a good school. We planned on having a baby years ago… we tried so hard.

I began to give up, thinking I was barren and suddenly one day Talib told me that we had to pack up and move.

"There are too many people here." He said.

So we fled into an area where the houses were all at least 20 miles away from each other. Talib and I aren't shy, but we've been in several situations that no one should witness—I didn't question our sudden change of plans.

However, I was stressed about my own shortcomings, and one night, in our new house, I cried out to him, "I'm barren, aren't I?"

He looked at me, startled by my question, "How should I know?"

"Well, that's why we moved here, isn't it? You have lost all hope in me, and you don't want us to be by the schools."

In a jolt of emotions, I flopped onto the bed like a sad, dead fish and sobbed very silently.

"Aina!" He shouted at me, "Wonder, you're very upset, I can tell."

"Oh! Did you figure that out, genius?" I said angrily, sitting up and abruptly coming face-to-face with him.

"Love," He said, calmly (he was always so calm. It truly amazed me.)

"Love," he kissed me softly, "I know we've been trying to have a child, and you're hurting. I don't believe you're barren though, and no, I haven't given up on you. I actually think you're," he paused, "pregnant—kind of."

He said that smiling, and then chuckled a little.

I only became more upset with him, "All that tells me is that you think I've gotten 'kind of' fat!" I whined.

Talib and I both looked at my flat stomach and laughed.

"But what do you mean?" I said after the giggles stopped.

"Eh… Ahh, um, we'll I'm not certain about anything yet, I just know that you're beginning to look different again."

I knew what that meant, but then he corrected my quote-unquote "knowledge".

"By 'different' I don't mean sickly," he said, referring to the deathly sickness I overcame centuries ago, "I mean… you've got a *glow* about you."

I grinned.

"Yes." He grinned with me, "It's exciting, but I don't believe it's your *average* pregnancy glow."

He meant that the "glow" had magical properties. And I nodded.

Then—one month later, on that near-to-last unpacking day, I thought of what he had said several weeks ago, and my eyes widened as I turned back to look at my project.

In that moment, as I realized what must've been happening. I noticed that his crossed arms were actually cradled, so I jumped up abruptly and followed him into our slightly-prepped baby room.

I figured he must've been having a vision, or something of the like.

As I watched, he placed an invisible (to me) babe in our basinet, and as soon as he turned to me, and I saw some tears in his eyes, I ran and jumped up into those strong, handsome arms.

"Oh, my god… darling. If you could only see her. She's so beautiful…"

I wiped my eyes, "Her?" I said, breaking from our embrace, "We're having a baby girl?"

I smiled.

"We have one." He whispered.

I ogled the basinet in sheer astonishment.

"Well, not completely yet." He corrected himself, "The tharpels are still weaving themselves together."

My eyebrows were raised in perplexity, and that was when he first explained tharpels to me and how—with our help—they created our daughter.

"When I told you to keep your eyes open," he later explained, "the tharpels were streaming from your gaze and into my arms." He said they'd gathered our 'scent', essence, and D. N. A.

"This is so strange," I said, marveling, "I *will* be able to see her, won't I?"

I dreaded the thought of an invisible child, but I prepared myself for it.

"Well, of course. She's got your blood in her! *Human* blood. To the best of my knowledge, two fourths of her is made up of you and me. The other half of her D.N.A. is composed completely of tharpels.

"Somehow they must've traveled with me while I was in Husrodolg, and then infiltrated my thoughts and wanted to help us have our baby."

I smiled at him. I've asked him to describe to

me their features, but he said he couldn't find the words. And yes, I've asked him why I couldn't see them.

"They can't cloak themselves from eyes that have seen their homeland. And, well... I *have.* And you, my Aina, have not."

... So the magical spirits remained a mystery to me, like much of Talib's life.

My husband was a traveler, and I was just not the type. I loved to explore, but remotely, maybe through say: a downtown area, or some shops. Although, in our time together, he'd sweep me off my feet and take me along to his beloved distant lands anyway. But never to Husrodolg.

Anyway, this story belongs to Joslin...

The tharpels constructed her like cells would a normal human body. They were strongly bonded to one another, sewn together by their spirit "thread". Born of the same place and person, yet still capable of independent flight; they were an intricate part of Joslin's being.

I had my mixed feelings about them. While my husband could be at peace, unafraid and loving toward every magical property he could see in Joslin, I was bothered by these creatures. I knew that they technically *were* my daughter, but I couldn't wrap my mind around that fact when I was breast-feeding her, or teaching her to walk.

Most of the time, I felt like they were an incurable disease. To me, they were a plague on my daughter that I couldn't control.

Yet, I could dismiss those thoughts, because Talib said that the tharpels were harmless, and even helpful. He knew more about the creatures than I did. He knew their powers and their gifts.

He'd been to their world.

When I said "my wizard of a man," I wasn't joking. Talib knew magic.

Talib, however, didn't know much about little girls. So, when my baby grew, I nurtured her princess-like side, and made sure she could have an average enough human life.

She was only five months old when Talib told me some very upsetting news.

He said to me, "Aina, I'm sure I mentioned long ago: tharpels cannot be controlled."

I looked at him crossly as I finished tending to a messy Joslin who had potato smashed into her nose and was managing to half laugh, half cry.

15

"What do you mean? We can't figure out how to stop the tharpels from changing her? We must have some kind of trap for them when they rip her apart. Little demons."

"Darling, first off, they don't rip her apart. It's only happened once where they've separated, and they were just curious about the house. They can't explore as much as a human baby. Second, they're not evil. Love, you're forgetting that they're a big part of her."

"I am not! I'm reminded **every day**. This is why she's essentially in exile!" I said, triumphantly wiping the last bit of snot-mixed potato off her face.

Talib ignored my effortless rebuttal, "Indeed, dear, there is no way to tell, or be certain that Joslin wouldn't transform into the invisible spirits, say during recess or while she's in a detention later-on…"

"Oh," I giggled, "You're no detention baby, are you?" I said to my little angel's chubby face, "No you're not. No, no, no, you are not!"

Talib forfeited his concentration on our serious topic. He crossed his eyes and started mocking my baby voice. And I completely busted out laughing.

I mean, okay, imagine this man; looks to be about in his twenties, so tall that his head hits the ceiling easily—and he's ripped.

When I say ripped, imagine crazy muscles—leaner than a bodybuilders, tough enough to notice when relaxed. My husband—this stud—is in a three-piece suit and he is crossing his eyes and mocking my "baby voice" almost perfectly.

It was quite the sight to see to say the least.

Anyway, due to our lack of control over her, we kept Joslin in the house. We never let her leave. Our plan was to homeschool her, and then we'd see if one day she could possibly control the spirits on her own.

We kept her away from the view of others so that no one could ever discover these creatures that she hid within her physical guise of a human body.

Joslin knew nothing of these creatures, or that any secrets existed in her house. She was accustomed to her enclosed surroundings and happy with our little secret life, unaware that being hidden from the world was abnormal.

Talib and I both knew that she was special, and different. Our lives were changed and my entire existence I devoted to my incredible daughter…
■■

Joslin's memoirs:

The small white creatures touched my skin. They danced a ballet into my pores and swarmed about infecting my blood...

The creatures were a part of me; they weren't magic nor were they the maggots that they portrayed. They were something to construct me.

I'm made of these.

(But I can't be...)

I woke.

Mother perched a narrow hip at my bedside to greet me as her routine dictated. This day was the first birthday that my memory kept (my third one). More importantly, this day marked my introduction into what I call "spiritual knowledge", which radiated through me since then for the next two years.

Unlike Talib (my father), mother knew my likes and dislikes.

Mother knew, for example, that I didn't want to be that little child who drooled on her chest and couldn't use the toilet. She knew that I had greater ambition than that.

On this lovely morning, I still proved to be that same eager child who knew more than she should, and still couldn't know enough.

I knew the whole potty-training thing, and mastered it. I knew how to brush my teeth, wash myself, my hair, and put my clothes on right. I even knew how to walk into a room with grace and determination.

The grace in movement had been taught by my father, for as beautiful as Mother was, she had absolutely no grace.

Father used to disappear and was gone more often than not, but he must've taught me grace somehow, for my mother knew nothing of it. Aina taught me many things, but most things, I just learned on my own.

*She wished that I would learn fast, and she wanted me to be the brightest child in the world, but, as I gathered later on, from the writings in my father's old and sacred journal, she didn't anticipate **or** appreciate my speed.*

She'd laugh and ask me to "Slow down!" randomly and I didn't understand it at the time.

My father, however, in the moments he spent with me, supported my growth and saw nothing but excitement in my abnormal learning rate. On my second birthday, Father taught me how to read at a first grade level; my erudition enticed him.

My teeth grew in seemingly all at once and I could annunciate whatever word sat on a page. Since that day, Talib gave me a vocabulary lesson whenever he saw fit.

At this age of three, I came to the point where I could carry on in an adult conversation with my cute, minuscule toddler's voice.

On my third birthday, I was ready to be the best pupil for my father and mother.

Alas, despite my urge to seize this day with all my birthday wishes, Aina spoke discouraging words that morning. I could hear their vague presence hanging about the air the moment she spoke, "Little angel?"

She spoke my pet name in a question as if she'd be wondering soon if I was okay. I nodded as I watched sweet pixie dust flutter through her eyes, agonized underneath the weight of the information she withheld.

"Your father is going to be…"

… out of town for today…

That was the horrid news I knew so well.

Before she could even finish her sentence, my head hung low and I slouched over my feet and groaned.

Father took away the only birthday present I wanted from him ever since I looked into his eyes for the first time after leaving the womb. That might be an exaggeration, but I honestly feel as though it's one hundred percent true.

*"On any other day, his actions would've been remotely acceptable." I said to my worried mother, "but I love him and I want him with me… and today was supposed to be **mine**."*

I felt that ripping feeling between my heart (which needed to hold him close) and my mind (which knew of his need to provide for us.)

■■■

As the present beckons her back to reality, Joslin notices that the car she's been riding in has passed the sign that welcomes travelers into Alabama. Her body moves in discomfort, torso adjusting and then her hips until she finally sighs and unplugs the seatbelt digging into her narrow side.

She rubs the sore spot with her fingers and slowly brings her pale legs up to claim a fetal position to comfort herself.

Scents of sooty mold and magnolia dance in the air, and remind her of the heart and soul of the area around her. The land that Alabama was named for carries an air as sweet as Georgia peaches and as bitter as dusty roads. The roads leading to her second hometown make the air sour like a spoiling green worm.

Inside the car, via peripheral vision, she sees the back of her Jamaican-looking driver, and a mouth in the rearview mirror moving 30-miles-a-minute with southern tones. The movements of her lips are comical, because of how wide the vowels yawn in such a short amount of time. Joslin finds that in her daze, she can't even recognize the words.

In the passenger seat are suitcases and boxes belonging to her driver, Miranda, and in the seat next to Joslin are her own suitcases.

Joslin rolls her eyes at herself wondering why she's in the situation she's in. *I thought I left this place for good, forever.*

"I won't remember this ghost town." She states in a whisper with her eyes clouded, "Not yet... as long as I can hold it off."

So instead of gazing upon the physical reminders outside of her window, she closes her eyes to erase them and forces her memories farther back to her fantastical childhood once again:

My little feet were fumbling still in the morning, despite my gracefulness. (Which I'd pride myself on every day).

My mother bit her lip as we walked through the widespread hall of bedrooms. A worry line furrowed her brow while she thought of a way to make my birthday fabulous without her husband to help her.

She succeeded with flying colors, however simple she thought her distractions to be.

On my third birthday my mother taught me the arts of dance! The beginning of the lesson started with a liquid-like motion of her hand, demonstrating spirit and life. She really only set her chin upon her palm as I ate my breakfast quickly, but somehow, I remember it looking so passionate.

Her eyes held me in their view with endearment unlike any I'll ever see again.

The whole time she kept me thinking about how incredible it was to have someone so incredible think that I was so... well... incredible... Let's just say that I admire a true mother's love.

Aina was insanely beautiful, inside and out. Her physical traits didn't cover half of her outward beauty. The way she presented them...

When she walked, it was more like she was stepping in and out of puddles on a rainy day, clumsy and smooth at the same time. Her every action incarcerated a beauty to behold.

Eventually, after thinking about my luck (you know, having a faerie for a mother and all that) it was time for the activity of the day.

First, Aina told me the reasons I should start practicing the thing she called a sport. She told me about it in her usual listing technique she'd use while teaching, "It seems, my dear, that I've been learning to dance for thousands of years," she stated... and of course, instantly, I was intrigued.

She continued, "I've learned ballet from Jules Cardinal Mazarin, ballroom from your father, tap from Bill Robinson, and jazz, shuffles and folkdances from various groups." She laughed at that impossible collection.

"Joslin, I believe you should have lessons immediately for something that I may have accidentally tattooed to your DNA. The way you move about proves to me every day that you're more than ready."

*"Well, today hasn't really been my most **graceful** of days..." I stated, blushing, seeking out more attention.*

"On a different note, I shall also teach you to cook if you wish." She beamed excitedly, ignoring my comment.

I nodded as quietly as I usually did for my father, because the concentration I wanted should not have been broken by my own words.

Despite my efforts to create silence, giggles and sighs of laughter soon filled the room as our performances began.

The movements from my feet were like responses to the twirl of the earth. Dance was a form of art, art was a form of love, and I felt love all around me.

We counted at first: "1 and 2, 3 and 4..."

And eventually I had a rhythm down for mostly every dance I'd been taught.

Aina, the clumsily-beautiful dancer, and her graceful beginner glided around the hard wood floor with feet lighter than the wings of a hummingbird.

When the dancing lessons were over, I felt my feet become the extension of my soul. They moved like the speech from a Southern pastor's voice, without the words, and the rest of my body followed in song like a choir as my heart thumped like their clapping hands.

The reality of physical magic began drowning our personas in this thickly flowing warm-blooded passion for movement. My entire being sunk into the ideology of dance.

*My toes learned to point and tap and swoosh without messages from my brain. They felt solidified, and independent, as if they were a part **of** me apart **from** me.*

When my body could no longer quench my soul of its thirsting desire to move, it collapsed on the sofa facing a blank wall.

I drank from a water glass that Aina hastily retrieved from the kitchen. My heart and mind were reconnected with my body after its shocking encounter with my youthful soul.

I lifted my feet onto the couch like a footrest plopping my head down on the floor with my swimming blood moving toward my brain.

I glowered at my tiny piglet-looking toes, and then grinned. So thankful for them that I wanted to kiss each one, so I began to stretch. My lips were puckered, so I suppose I must've looked silly.

"Good!" mother said, entering the room.

Startled, I looked up at her quickly, and she just grinned, "Stretching helps your muscles stay in shape!

You'll be dancin' even better than you been dancin', my sweet angel."

The compliment **had** to be my best present by far!

Yet, the day put perspective into my system as well. I proved to be an awful cook, and the worst part was the klutzy way I did things around the kitchen.

I usually walked gracefully, smiled in a way that swans may have envied for its grace, and I showed even more elegance and sureness while I danced earlier that day. My spirits sank slightly when I realized that I wasn't a gifted cook.

Mother had to remind me that I was "only three, after all," but as she did, I protested her excuse:

"Mother, if I am able to do certain things that astonish both you and father at my age, I should be able to do **anything** now."

Aina took me by the hand and led me into the den. As she sat herself on the couch, she lifted me onto her lap and sighed with her eyes glistening in earnest. Her locket necklace (which was more of a limb than an accessory) glimmered a happy faded orange color within the creases of the design.

She lifted our lightweight throw-blanket over both of our heads, and kissed my forehead. Her necklace's light became more prominent, but as she readjusted, it did not move like a normal necklace would. It leeched onto her skin, unable to move freely.

This always left me distracted, and often, as my mother talked, I would look from her eyes, to her locket charm, and then to her mouth in a repetitious cycle.

"Angel, there happens to be not one single person alive who can perform every obstacle and learn every lesson in life with ease."

"Until I came along," I gloated. I didn't realize that gloating about things was seen as an ignorant gesture and only disproved my own words.

"Joslin... no. It doesn't matter how angelic a person is. Especially if one is so young and undeveloped, they cannot be perfect. Even those of us who don't believe in imperfections are imperfect (and mainly the reasons revolve around our own disbeliefs)."

She lifted the blanket, smooched my forehead, and hopped into the kitchen to create the homemade spaghetti lunch that I failed making the dessert for.

My eyes spaced off into the wall opposite from where we'd sat. I felt little compartments in my heart and mind storing this lesson. I savored the sound of each word, but understood little of it. I thought of the ignorance I had as an "imperfect perfection" and I enjoyed that contradiction.

My spirits drained the day after: Another sunny day and my father didn't show.

Sadly, at that point, I never saw my father except in glimpses and fractions of time during my third and fourth year of life. I began to think of him as a fantasy creature that I'd made up in my head or a figment of my imagination whenever he did come around.

He only emerged from hiding to greet me goodnight when I should've been asleep already and I only saw him clearly in the pictures and paintings on some of our walls in the hallway. Every day during that time, Aina's step was unnaturally slow and careful as opposed to her usual cheerful and clumsy persona.

I tried being happy, but the state of things continued past my fourth birthday. He missed each holiday that year, including my fourth Christmas. He missed my fourth birthday and my fifth.

One day in March, after I'd been five for about two months, Aina left home to go shopping. After two months of becoming accustomed to Talib's bastardy habits, I received an unusual greeting:

"Good morning, butter-nose!"

Talib grinned at my hazy expression and I brought him into focus. I blinked twice, cocked my head sideways and frowned.

Then I grinned wider than he.

"Oh, Father!" I shouted, "I knew you were real!"

My body quivered gently in his arms as I embraced him all too suddenly. Tiny tears made my cheeks moist and my eyelashes startled my eyes when I blinked.

So, my body quivered in short hiccups and gasps until I managed to calm myself and look at the man I'd been deprived of. He was very different... well, not to an extreme, but I was worried for only a moment that I was mistaken in all of my assumptions. My father now had five deep scars on his face, and two on his shoulder, and his eyes were sunken in slightly from a lack of sleep that I didn't understand at the time.

He was my father though. As pale as the vampires and polar bears in storybooks and as tall as our house level would comfortably allow him to be. I admired the vision I had of him and couldn't resist giggling faintly as he spoke. His words passed softly to me and his hands held tightly to me, cradling me dearly.

"Joslin, I promise you, I will never leave you for as long as I left you, ever again. I'll hold you close to me in my heart, as I cling to your heart wherever you go. Every *morning, I will do my best to show you exactly how much I love you." When he finished I realized that I had been sobbing uncontrollably. This speech was the first and only from Talib that I could ever whole heartedly believe.*

■■

Through a dash of ageless light confined within twists and turns of different shades of green, Talib Tilda's eyes glimmered. In his perspective, today was a gift and the gift lasted for eternity. He always seemed to be someone who had lived forever.

Talib charmed society in the many different ways he knew the Earth. It seemed that there was no human alive that couldn't be persuaded into everything he said. He would think in a way that most people never dreamed of thinking.

Yet, Joslin didn't even know this about him until five minutes ago when she read the first page of his old brown journal.

He had never let the parchment out of his sight until the night he died and it took her twelve years to finally open it. As she sits, still riding in the back of that same car, she reads on, into the descriptions of his family, and starts to think, again, about the past. She thinks about how much she really misses him...

I crawled up like a ladybug, circling around my father's lap. My braided hair bobbled like antenna and my toes moved like feelers. In my imagination, I had this rough exoskeleton, built for dominance, endurance and protection. Within my mind I became as cute as a ladybug and tough as a horned beetle.

The timing of my story is now the March or April past my fifth birthday. I turned 5 in January. Talib and I had formed wonderful traditions.

We read at least two books a day. The old pages of the fantasy books he read charmed me. With the dust of ancient lives, the stories rang mysterious and thought-beckoning in my brain.

Every book we had was "used". People had read the pages and finished their lives leaving an essence on this lasting storybook. The words bringing the books to life admired their own details, treating them like lovers. The ink caressed the pages with meaning so passionately, that they came together perfectly.

Hands and fingers of people I'll never know pinched each of those pages. Their souls were lost in the same book that my father would soon lead me into.

I felt the spirits of one thousand minds or more enter my head. Excitement crept up in through the waters running in my blood. The emotion danced and made ripples, awakening my limbs with the rupture of my brain's ecstatic waves.

My father was about to teach!

Whether he composed this lesson of new vocabulary or new stories or even facts about the world around me, the feeling of my nerves rattling consumed me. Anything he spoke of would be fine, as long as I could fill some of the void of wonderment trapping my mind into numbness.

Today, Talib Tilda, my wise old father, opened the great binding of a book known to be a member of the fantasy genre.

"Sometimes, Joslin," he said, marveling at my enthusiasm, "These books marked 'fantasy' are in fact by their definition, 'the writings of a world invented in the author's mind'. However, others marked like this are true stories with a false genre placed on them due to their peculiarity. I warn you now to not take this book in as falsehood."

I nodded in response, almost wishing to yell, "Alright, alright, go on and read to me before I turn six!" but I halted the words, remembering that they were impolite. Still, although I only nodded, I did so vigorously, constantly thirsting for the words that I wanted him to read.

Sure, I could've started reading it on my own, but what's the fun in that? Father did the character voices perfectly, and even if it was just a narrative, he read the novels with the greatest of intrigue and candid delivery for each phrase.

He continued to explain to me nonetheless, "This story is completely true, butter-nose." He said, his deep voice causing small goose bumps to form in my suspense, "Someday, you will meet the characters in this book and you must be prepared to befriend them."

I nodded ever so forcefully, feeling that my neck muscles might be sprained.

What would this story be?

I didn't know and I didn't care, I just wanted to hear. I listened intently, although I refused to believe a word that he said.

For a child, I had a strong sense of doubt. The only things I believed to be absolute truths came from my mother's lips.

On with the story, which spoke of wizards and a banished princess, faeries and witches, and grass dragons. He finished the two chapters he'd promised to read and left me, once again, in suspense.

He told me to disregard the genre marking on that book, but how could I? He said that the information was vital to me, but stopped reading in order to leave me in suspense, whereas if the words were true, I was sure he'd make sure that I received the information.

Instead he simply set it down, saying, "More later," just like he would for any faerie tale.

Again, I was unable to trust him completely, and although I trusted him to never leave again, I didn't believe he told me the truth about anything really.

Unlike Talib, my mother always remained constant and true. The fact of the matter came to be that my father could prove himself an honest man to everyone except me.

Aina, my pixie-like mother, woke me every morning and put me to sleep every night. If father didn't show, she would, and if she didn't, father wouldn't be there either. (They only left me alone when I should've been sleeping.)

What resulted from that of course: I saw my mother's face more, and every reaction and movement she made around me. As a natural result of deprivation from the man, my mother gained more trust from her daughter than Talib ever could.

Still, although less energetic and child-like than Aina, Talib allowed me more intrigue than my mother did most of the time.

I didn't like to play house or go on playgrounds or eat candy foods while socializing. The activities listed seemed to be my mother's specialties, and they were the things she thought I ought to do.

But, I only wanted to learn all the knowledge in the world.

*For pleasure, I picked up lessons from father and anything else that my experience and imagination could teach me. Father provided me with what I **needed** and that was my kind of fun.*

Still, only as a five-year-old did I know my father, and still he was known as "the business man type". His trips took precedence over his daughter.

I do remember a few weeks he had off. Time to heal from "work-related injuries". (I still don't know exactly where he worked, or what kind of work he could've done to receive the injuries). Talib and I had lots of fun for those weeks. Those days to heal were the last we spent together.

We'd stay up late each night, eating ice cream as he read ghost stories and other fantasies to me. (Mother didn't have quite the same gift with dialogue as he did, and she didn't like me staying up so late, but father would argue that they only had so much time to spend with me, and he was very right.) ... (He would never know just how right he was...)

Sometimes, Talib didn't understand me, and reading to me helped him, if only just a little.

Joslin thinks for a while about her past until she can take it no longer, and she has to write about it. She wants to speak about it, but not to her driver. So she begins a heavy scrawling in her father's journal:

He would raise one eyebrow as I laughed hysterically and he'd say, "Joslin, I fail to see how this is funny... the man just got beheaded!"

We were reading an old story that my father found unpublished, dated all the way back to 1890. The storyline was strange for that age of literature.

In summary, it involved an old man who had a shabby toothed smile and a very fickle wife. A curse overtook him and his skin started melting over time, reducing him to a mere living skeleton. He was angry because he couldn't feel anything.

He was also enraged because his wife no longer loved him at all. He went to a ballroom one night and saw his wife dancing with another man. He drew his sword quickly and sliced the man's head clean off.

Now, the first time my father read this to me, I was rather bothered. The idea of someone melting scared me and made me feel vulnerable, as if I were a part of the story. I cried myself to sleep in a panic of thoughts.

This action caused my mother to scold father the next morning. Since then, I thought about it and I never truly finished the story. I couldn't have an unfinished mystery, and I wasn't all too creative (just full of wonder).

So I begged my father to read it again, and after about ten minutes he said, "Alright, Joslin, I shall read it to you again, but if you get scared, you tell me."

You can imagine that he was astonished when I wouldn't stop laughing. I giggled until my face turned a very pinkish color, and then realized that an explicating statement of clarification was in order.

My explanation for him was as follows: "Truly, father, it was obvious that the man was going to be beheaded. He was asking for it, provoking the demon-man with glances and taunting him. Furthermore, I question the entire story's legitimacy. God wouldn't let that skeleton man live in the first place. He's got no blood, and you need blood to live, among other various parts, such as organs..."

So, my father turned out to be the one who couldn't stop laughing that night.

The way I spoke was exceptionally better than any five-year-old should have been able to, but it was simply the way I had been taught. He remarked in his journal about that night, saying "an adult's voice spoke clearly from a five-year-old's body." His words made me sound a little creepy.

My mother and father had taught me anything and everything I could possibly fit into my brain at the time. Grammar and speech were easy to learn. Talib taught me grammar and written word, while my mother was just an excellent speaker.

—OH and how I miss my mother! Not only was she intelligent, but she was beautiful like a faerie. I always thought she was a faerie. She was slender and brightly colored, and very, very short.

My mother wasn't so much of the "angel" type. She was far too mischievous, and always held a gleam of trouble in her eyes. Her very presence looked for mischief, and her actions were spontaneous.

She let me know that it was okay to mess with the order of things as long as I didn't get caught. It always made me smirk and giggle. How I loved my mother's beautiful treachery!

2154

Her hand begins to ache, so Joslin sets the pen down and now looks out into the world outside of the car, moving fast and closer to their destination. She continues her thoughts, her eyes narrowed on the blurry, ever-shifting foreground beyond the foggy window.

2141

Aina held me like any mother should and giggled in the same octaves as I did. She understood me when I was scared and smirked at me when I did wrong.

Her beauty was erratically erotic and beautifully strange, and it fit into our house more than anything. She took the time for us to feel an essence of home breathe in the very foundation of each wall, and when the lights came down, there was no fear—no nightmares ever.

She lit up my thoughts and decorated my world with her life and her light and her spirit.

My father described her beauty as a divine art as if she were some sort of goddess instead. He told me that whenever my mother blinked, ten-thousand angels sang in a faerie language above our level of hearing. He said that when she walked, his heart would swim into his throat and beat slowly. Her breath, he said, was the song of a miracle.

I always called him silly for saying such things. His words were always so poetic. They knew no other formations save for the quixotic.

He was a romantic, constantly describing her as an angel with brilliant pixie dust eyes. He saw her only for what she was... what I saw her to be.

My parents would roam around the house, distant, then pass by each other and startle up a flame that I couldn't recognize at the time. Aina strutted in her rickety flutter of a walk and he would instantly sweep her off of her feet.

When I would watch them circling around the

rooms, I felt like we were all on a ballroom floor.

Two people who lived like normal humans became immortal just by swinging each other around. The admiration glistened on their skin and shimmered near their fingertips while their hands held on for dear life. My father seemed to be the most handsome man in the world, and the woman he held... well, she was radiant.

She was, in fact, very beautiful (I'm not sure if I could ever say that enough). One thing I knew for sure was that she didn't need any of her glittery make-up. Still, it clouded around her eyes making them light up brighter each time she'd blink.

They were an intense and ever-pressing blue like that of the most radiant skies. If you looked closely enough, you could see light grey clouds moving along her irises as if stolen from a stormy sky.

She had ebony hair (attributed as well to me) and a French woman's figure and the tiniest feet I had ever seen aside from my own of course, but hers were only an inch larger than her five-year-old daughter's.

Talib convinced my mother to always keep one thing a mystery to me.

"She'll find out when she's older," He'd say on the subject. "Either we shall tell her, or they'll let her know."

I overheard this, and similar words about the same subject time and time again.

What was this thing that I ought to have known?

I only knew with what it must've had to do:

At the back of Aina's neck always sat a golden latch which held the gold chain of a locket necklace in place. The charm of the locket was a flattened gold circle with reddish-gold feathering on the front.

In the center was a key hole, which looked to be the exact fit of the two reddish gold key earrings that she always wore as well. There was something special about the locket, aside from the fact that it was nearly as wondrously stunning as the lady who wore it.

When my mother would smile, the center of the charm started glowing bright gold.

When she was upset, it would glow a bright and eerie yellow.

To us it wasn't strange. Still, people came to the door to drop off boxes and other things and they more-than-noticed it. After a few incidents, I began to wonder...

Once, a deliveryman came with a box of fantasy books. (We could never get enough fantasy books; for me the interest was hereditary.)

My mother told him to come inside right away because he looked as if he would fall over with the weight of the box.

He set it down on the couch and gave her a clipboard to sign.

While her pen scurried along on the paper, the man's eyes were riveted on the locket that hovered above her breast.

I stared at him, confused.

His smarmy hands were sweating, and he kept swallowing a lump in his throat. He looked as though he had never seen a locket shining like that. My mother looked up with a smile and then quickly looked down.

"Eh-Excuse me? Sir? Are you alright?"

"Uh, err, yeah." Said the man, "Miss, pardon my askin', where did you get that?"

"What, sir?" I remember how flustered my mom had been by the interrogation. She had a particular way of hiding it, but I could always tell.

"Why, that locket necklace... I swear it's lighting up just like yer face."

My mother beamed, "Why thank ya sir, and thank you for delivering this package, I wouldn't want to keep you here. Now bye!"

During that sentence, the man tried to talk but was halted in his acts each time. My mother shut the door fast behind him and slunk down to the floor.

I ran to her, "Mother, why's he so inter'sted in your locket."

She gritted her teeth slightly and squinted at me, "I don't know, Joslin, he's probably just never seen a locket glowing before."

"So, all lockets don't do that?"

"No, darling, your father made this locket special for me."

"It holds your powers right? Is that why the man couldn't hold it?"

She beamed at me, "Well, I'm sure he has other things to do besides hold other people's necklaces, Joslin. And what makes you think I have powers?"

"Because you're **my** mommy!" I said in cheer.

She smirked at me, and grabbed my sides, tickling me until I was red, "And **you're** just **so** special, hmm?" She shouted, grinning and laughing with me.

We settled on that point until that same night.

I didn't think of her secrecy as anything but a game: Aina was trying to hide her super powers so that I

38

could discover them on my own. She was fanning the flame; feeding the beast that was my curiosity.

I assumed she lied; Talib couldn't have made the necklace. I figured that Aina found it and just flung her powers into it, to store them so that she might appear more human-like than she actually was.

We both fell asleep together on the couch (Talib was "working" late that night and mother didn't want to be in her bed alone.) I woke up and examined her necklace. It had golden swirls like ocean waves that my fingertip surfed on for a moment.

I scooped it up softly into my left hand and suddenly (startling me) my mother woke up, gasping for air.

Her head became white and pale, with eyes sunken in slightly. As her eyes began to blacken, she grasped my hand and shook the locket from it.

I was nearly in shock, her look was so frightening. Before I let go though, I looked at the locket that was enveloping itself in black. Then, it fell back to her chest and beamed pink again.

My mother beamed along with it, breathing heavily, "Honey, don't touch this locket, okay?" It was the most serious tone that I had ever heard her voice carry.

I shrugged, "Okay, mommy."

∎∎∎

Currently, Joslin finds herself sitting in the backseat of a Bugatti Veyronnette (the only car model Joslin knew of over fifty years old making new models)... (Though, she wasn't well learned on cars in the first place). Her driver never shuts up and she finds irony in the fact that the car goes as fast as Miranda's mouth (O-60 in .5 seconds).

What brings Joslin's pondering, wandering mind to the past is not her talkative driver in the front seat, although she could be very distracting sometimes.

Some of the passages of her father's old journal get her thinking. Some are descriptive with nature and some about her mother. She would always have memories of her mother's loving traits, but she sometimes forgets how Aina's face looked before the incident of her murder. The journal helped her recall her mother's beauty.

Then the written works on nature give Joslin a peaceful feeling towards the present. She read about her father's discoveries as if he were a second Thoreau. He wrote poems about how the moon connected with the sky and how the sun embedded its light into the clouds. He wrote about the trees and their seasons, and how even in dormancy they seemed to be alive and vibrant, like human hands scratching at the wind.

And Joslin writes:

My father was composed slightly differently than mother and I. He was a tall man, bone-thin and best described to have the look of a ghost, but he was definitely not frightening.

My mother called him a wizard, but I couldn't see that. All the wizards I'd heard of were old and haggard.

Talib was fit and his skin was taut on his face— not a wrinkle in sight. Just strong arms and a strong chin. His eyes were the deep emerald of some of the nature he observed, and his skin was ivory. He passed those latter traits to me: my green eyes and paper white skin.

My mother had the skin of a porcelain doll, not quite so pasty looking, and she had given me my black hair, pointed ears, and my tendency to be overly skinny.

Father had a silence that not even the coldest lands of the arctic could mock. I remember that it was the only thing that mother was opposed to with him. He hardly ever talked to me, except to tell me he loved me and call me silly nicknames like "cupcake" or "butter-nose". Or, of course, to read stories to me even though I could read on my own.

When it was time for me to go to sleep, my father would take my face in both hands, kiss me on the nose and say, "Sleep tight, butter-nose."

He said those things sometimes, but mostly he just held onto me and gave me his warmth in his hugs.

Still, I never saw father at the breakfast table. He only walked by it. He always wore a suit like the major businessman that he happened to be.

*There was nothing thrilling about Talib. All I could see was a soft mysterious presence, and random professionalism. When mother walked by him, though, she had an extra spin in her step. I'm sure that if she **were** a faerie, her wings would flutter when they kissed. My mother must've loved him for the mysteries in his head, but I was unsure.*

The thing that I remember most about him was his deep, soft voice, and his most prized possession was this small brown book, which he held onto always.

It had tatters and tears in the cover and I always wondered why he loved it so much... it was the only book in our house that I was not allowed to look inside of. (This of course burdened my curious mind)

Finally, after all of those years, Joslin reads into his book, which teems with a whispered penciled-font of mysteries that she longs to unravel. Her eyes deviate from corner to corner, savoring the sight of each stressed stretch of lead against paper.

Disembodied, the lines are simplistic and chaotically happy (as scribbles always are).

Together, the lines are complicated, complex and passionate; transforming always from letters into words, from words into sentences, from sentences into thought, and from there the thoughts became portals.

The portals are a connection, where Joslin can see her father (although he cannot see her). Different portals are made for different sprees of imagination—moments when she can envisage his reactions and envision his truths.

She turns page after page, finding descriptions of her mother and herself. He could depict each of their personal characteristics so well; it amazes her how he truly thought that they were both magical.

The idea used to be an instinct for Joslin to believe herself, but her better judgment relays the notion as false. Yet— if her father thought of it too, it may not have been too far from the truth even if she had a hard time trusting him; Talib was never a foolish man.

As she continues to delve into the pages of the journal, Joslin notices an obsession over her mother's name. It was a quirk that Talib had which was nothing short of ridiculous.

"Aina" was written over and over again. Whenever he scrawled about her thoughts, or her smile, or her body, he always spelled out her name. It was as if pronouns didn't even exist. She was certainly his enchantress......

Joslin writes once again:

The last week of April... 2142

I REMEMBER THAT MORNING… THE MORNING EVERYTHING CHANGED. IT SEEMED THAT I HAD AWAKENED FROM A BEAUTIFUL DREAM. **WHEN THE DAY WAS OVER, REALITY WAS MY FATE…** BUT BEFORE THE SLEEP LEFT MY EYES, THE DAY STARTED.

Of course, I remember every word and action that destiny allowed me...
■■■
Joslin ceases her writing. Warm tears slip down her cheeks and crawl into the corners of her mouth. She hears her mother's voice so clearly in her head; it's as if she's back in time.
■■■
"Hey, little angel, get up." My mother said to the five-year-old me.

I smiled up at the grinning woman perched on the side of my bed. Her black hair rolled down on her shoulders and her bright blue-grey, faerie dust eyes squinted at me as she beamed.

The curls of black strands bobbled about in the air as she hopped off of the bed, stumbling slightly on her own foot and catching balance in the last second.

This would happen a lot for the tipsy-turvy pixie, and by that point, of course, I expected it.

It was still amusing, though, so I giggled softly and yawned.

After a while, I hopped up to my feet on my bed and down to the floor. We walked hand-in-hand to the kitchen; my mother and her shrunken twin tagging along like a little shadow. I sat in the oak chair across from her usual sitting place.

The table was still above my head.

I got down and grabbed the phone book from the box of books on our floor. I walked back only to run into a boulder of a leg.

Talib ruffled my hair as I said, "'Scuse me, father."

Talib nodded and as he smiled, he sat on the kitchen counter. I set the phone book down on the chair, climbed up, and started pouring syrup on the waffle that my mother had hastily plopped down onto my plate.

"Remember honey," she sang excitedly, as Father picked her up by the waist and held her on his lap, "We're having our family picnic in a few minutes!"

I hiccupped, nodded, and drank my glass of orange juice in a gulp.

I started walking slowly to my room until my father patted me on the butt, which meant, "Make haste," or "Move it, kid." And the latter usually had one of those toothy grins added afterward. I waited for one, but upon seeing no lifted lip; I just skipped down the hall.

I moved around hastily in my room. I took off my blue pajamas with spangled pink stars, sticky from the orange juice that dribbled off of my chin.

I put on my green shirt, then my pants and my right and left shoes. I ran out to greet my parents and my father laughed. My mother fixed my shoes and put them on the correct feet. I must've been so excited that I switched them around!

I hopped up and got into my jacket. I looked up at my skyscraper father and smiled. (It was the first time I saw him without a suitcase in the morning light.) He scooped me up into his warm arms and...

▪▪▪

2154

Joslin stops thinking for a moment; her eyes glaze over.

She wrote all she could remember of that day and now feels tears nearing the edges of her eyes. She wipes them collectively with her sleeve.

She remembers the day after that... Though the thoughts are hurtful, the only reason she was in the car in the first place was because of **that day**... It seemed to be the day that led to everything... the lift-off, the turning point of her entire life.

She was **only** *five*.

I opened my eyes to a blank white blur.

Sounds came, tiny beeps and buzzes and a ringing. I frowned, straining my eyes in confusion as I felt the ringing noise intensify and release in a rapid pattern within my head.

The blur came to focus and a man I had never seen before wore a green cap on his head and smiled down at me.

45

"Awake now I see, are we, little girl?" his deep tuba voice spoke to me.

I just stared at him, not knowing what to think. My mother said heaven was the best place I could go... I wasn't sure if I was there. She said it was as pure as pallid snow.

She didn't say it smelled like old people and she certainly didn't mention this unusual character.

I remember thinking about the most random things as the tall, black man with the green cap turned toward another man who just came in through the door.

They were nearly complete opposites in comparison... Maybe they were complete opposites:

The second man was very light skinned and completely bald. I was thinking in that moment that he must've been practicing that disgruntled and, frankly, pissed off face for a while. They muttered words too low for me to make out clearly.

Then the bald, ghastly man picked me up with ice-cold hands and held me in freezing arms and said, "I'll take care of her."

Then we left the smiley man in the room.

I started crying while we left and he glared—his pupils dark and eyes bloodshot.

I cried louder, wailing about as loud as I could. I did not know this strange man or why I was there in his strange arms. We managed our way out of the hospital and then he started talking to me.

"Okay, what's your name, tyke?" he said in irritation.

He dropped me to the cement and I ran to keep up with him as he was tugging my arm, "Joslin, Mr..." I breathed out between sobs.

"My name's Owen. I'm your uncle." He smiled, "And your parents" he paused, "...are dead."

Of course I was five and only knowing my parents, I didn't understand how being my uncle made him a relative, or what the word 'dead' truly meant, but I had an idea from the books my father read. So, my parents went to heaven and left me with this strange man...

He continued to explain as he lifted me up into the passenger seat of a grey pick-up truck, "You aren't gonna see them ever again, so I suggest when we go back to their house you take whatever you can. Death is harsh and cruel, kid, but it's real."

With that said Owen buckled me loosely into the seat and shut the door. My crying had stopped without me noticing and I stared at the windshield, my muscles relaxed, and my eyes disconsolate. I did not hear Owen go around the truck, I didn't hear him get in his seat or close the door. I didn't feel the monstrous motor of his truck kick in.

I didn't notice anything until we came up to my house. It had yellow tape all around it. You know those crime scene lines? I unbuckled, opened the door, and dashed to the house before Owen could even blink.

"Mother, Father!" I sang those words throughout the house.

They weren't in the den or their room or anywhere. Each time I looked somewhere they weren't, my cries grew louder. Then I started screaming until I could no longer breathe their names. I threw a fit of silence and whimpered softly until I got to the backyard.

Everything around me existed in slow motion once I saw two pale figures in the grass. I'm not-- quite sure how, but I made it past the policemen grabbing at me, past the wind pushing me back and streaming through my ears.

It was like an obstacle course to me, one that seemed to take forever to get through. The figures didn't move... but I recognized them.

I was still screaming their names and they didn't turn to me. There wasn't one twitch, one blink, or one small head lift. Suddenly I felt an overpowering feeling. It washed over me and felt like fire mixed with water sloshing around inside of me.

I felt alone... I'd never felt alone before.

The grass shuffled underneath my feet as they lightly pressed it down. I knelt at my father's body and tilted his head toward me. His skin was waned further than normal and his eyes were stones gazing through me. There was no warmth in his face and his suit was stained with blood. His dark brown hair was stained with blood as well and in those places were two deep bullet wounds. I kissed his cheek, sighing deeply, and ran to my mother.

I could hear the tones of her voice harmonizing with the wind. I could hear the sounds of the day before and her and father talking. I sat in the grass next to her broken body, her head facing away.

I turned her head and screamed. I thought to myself over and over again... the body I saw couldn't **possibly** be my mother, but it was.

"Mother! No! Why?" These words passed slowly, and softly. I wanted to scream. More and more I wanted to scream, but I couldn't.

Blood was leaking slowly from her open mouth even after however long she'd been there. Her blue eyes were blank white and sunken in, and yet they peered into me. She had a hand shaped bruise on her neck and a hole burned through where her locket should've been. Her green sundress was torn around the waistline and cuts lined up on her stomach.

I kissed her forehead and then wrapped my arms around her waist and cried. I felt a giant pain in my lungs, my heart and stomach. I think it's still there today...

I sobbed in slow motion for hours on end it seemed and a policeman finally dragged me away from the unhappy corpses. I sat on the porch as my sadness consumed me and watched the two policemen through squinting eyes and blurs of tears.

"That the lil' girl that bumped 'er head?" said one.

"Yeah," said another with a lighter voice, "Poor little child, it's not right to have this happen to you, not this young."

"Yeah, but the good thing is that she won't remember a thing when she's older, I hope she's got someone to look out for her."

That's when Owen came onto the porch nonchalantly, "I've got her from here, boys. Sorry 'bout that."

...Now, there's a point in every person's life when you realize that there are good people and bad people. I figured that out early. Good and evil... that's not just from the storybooks you find on the shelves; it's real.

Yes, I remembered most things from that time and they really changed my life. No, I did not have someone to look out for me. I figured that out early as well...

Owen stuffed a suitcase with some clothes and toys from my room. I picked up my father's precious book, which was still a mystery to me. Then I picked up the key earrings and chain to my mother's locket, which had vanished.

I put the keys in a random page and closed the book, then wrapped the chain around my neck. My ears weren't pierced. Mother always said no when I asked to get them pierced... So the earrings stayed in the book and I respected my mother's wishes.

Owen and I left the house that I had lived in my whole life. We rode in the car for a long time. Owen drove from Iowa's country-side into the backwoods rural areas of Alabama. During the eight rest stops I made him take, Owen became quite impatient.

He'd scream from outside the girl's restroom, "We have got to **go**, child!"

I did **not** appreciate his terms with me. The word "child" was quite belittling in these fearful moments. I felt different from a child in some way.

■■

For instance, I could manage not losing my sanity and that was more than any "child" could've done. He could simply recognize that.

I couldn't stay in his car long because it felt unsafe and I did not like Owen very much.

I formed a permanent routine after the fourth stop: After a while in the bathroom I would come out of a stall after crying a bit and convince myself that things would change for the better.

I would walk to the mirror looking down and wash my hands. When I looked up, that was the worst part of these stops because what should've been my reflection my dead mother's face.

Every time.

I ran out of the bathroom each time without

drying my hands and screamed into Owen's leg. My hands left dark spots on the light jean fabric, and tears left some as well.

He would pat my back with his freezing hands and say, "Okay, let's just get in the truck."

As we walked back, sometimes I'd look at his leg, at the tears I've cried. I hated them. They should not have even existed.

When I looked at the tears on his leg (it seems like a funny feeling to me now) but I was sure that it took up all of my strength right then not to explode into millions of pieces.

Aina's image seemed to follow me to every single mirror I saw. I was sure that my mother was living—half dead—inside of mirrors. My goal was to somehow get her out of there, or make things better. Maybe I could bring her back to life. I thought of those things during the car ride, just before I fell back to sleep.

I couldn't tell what he was saying but Owen screamed his heart out at me; giving me lectures about how to behave in public. I fell asleep to his shouting... I didn't care enough to even try to listen.

We were on the road for forever it seemed, and then we finally stopped.

I woke up for the final time when Owen shook me hard and said, "We're here."

I hopped out of the rusting doorway of the pick-up truck and landed on a dirt road with my black clip-on shoes, the soles last touched by my mother. The bare earth seemed like toxic waste on my faerie-touched shoes.

I sneered.

Owen grabbed my suitcase of clothes and a

51

random bag out of the back, walking swiftly, as if the world was right as rain and I walked behind up the stone-laid path to his black oak house.

The small door opened and the smell of Owen spread all along the house. I didn't know at the time but it was whiskey and beer combined with an old man's cologne and sweat and it just smelled awful.

Owen walked in and pointed to the staircase, "'K, yer room is any room upstairs. I don't care which. Ya can run around as much as ya wan' up there and make the biggest messes ya want."

Then he brought his face at eye level to me, "Don't ever you come into my study or the living room, you hear? If you wan' a snack er something you get it yer-self, in the kitchen right there."

He pointed to a small hallway with a refrigerator and other kitchen furnishings in it. Then he pushed me up on the first wooden step leading into darkness.

I paused there for a moment until Owen said, "Get on; get up there!"

With the brown book in my left hand and my suitcase in the right I struggled up the fifteen steps that led upstairs. When I got to the last step I dropped the suitcase at the top level and left it there.

There was a smell of rust and a feeling of worry in the very air around me.

I hugged my father's prized book to my chest and stepped forward. Every next step I took made the floor creak and I winced every time I heard it.

I managed to get to the first room on the left and open the black oak door that matched the floor and the rest of the house. I stepped inside and felt for a light switch on the wall, which I found under a spider's web.

The bulbs flickered on and a whole new world lit up in the small room.

The walls were painted orange and red roses seemed to dance on the black oak floor.

A twin bed sat crooked by the window just like the one I had at home except for its wonky placement. A faint smell of dust settling arose in the air, but it was comforting. I turned around to get my mother to help me clean but when I looked at the unfitting bleak and narrow hallway, my heart sank.

I held the old book tighter to my heart and shuffled my way forward so that the wood in the hallway wouldn't creak under me. I thought about the way mother laughed and called me her angel. I remembered our story nights and how father made me laugh when I was sad. I giggled just like before as I opened the next black oak door.

By the dim light coming from the first room, I could see that I was now in a laundry room. I never had heard of a laundry room upstairs. There they were, though: the washer and the dryer. In the corner were some empty baskets and then one full of jeans. I shut the door behind me as I stepped further on to the third door. I had to push this door to get it to even crack open.

Inside, blocking the door from opening all the way, were thousands of little toys and big toys alike. They were piled as high as my knees and covered up any sign of a floor being there. I let the door close, cowering for a few seconds, as it slammed shut. I figured the loud noise could trigger an unhappy meeting.

I was scared about Owen coming up the stairs, scared out of my wits. His demeanor was fine enough, but he frightened me. Also, aside from all that, he had come into my life as a harsh figure during a harsh time.

Owen didn't appear, but my investigation ceased anyway. I left the last two doors for later. For some reason, unbeknownst to me, there was a crack of light streaming from both of the rooms. Perhaps others lived here that I would meet later? I didn't know, but I shrugged, uncaring. They would be there in the morning after all if they existed.

I walked to the end of the hallway, grabbed my suitcase, and went in the first room. I picked up each rose. I figured out that they were false flowers, but that was okay, they seemed to brighten the room anyway. I set them on the dusty windowsill.

I stripped the mattress, patted some dust out, and dressed it with my sheet and blanket. I grabbed my little olive green bear and held it tight to my chest. I set it down on the bed and put on my pajamas, still sticky from my orange juice. Then I got into my bed and slept.

The only way to describe the dream I had that night is... demonic.

Interestingly, fear didn't strike until I awoke. I don't remember every detail because it was so long ago but I was walking with my mother and father... my dead mother and father. Their faces were staring into mine. Somehow, I thought it was because they wanted me to be with them, or I just wanted to be with them again... my flesh started tearing and I started bleeding from my eyes and mouth.

I woke up in the bathroom (which turned out to be through the fifth door) and the sight of my own reflection made me scream.

I ran downstairs and knocked on the wall before stepping into the living room. I tapped my fist many times without a response and grew impatient in about five seconds. I ran to the front of the easy chair where Owen *slept with a bottle of whiskey in his hand.*

I shook his arm and shouted in the midst of my crying, "Uncle Owen? I had a nightmare."

There was no response from the human lard. I made my next action, gripping my blanket tighter with my sweating hands. I climbed up onto my uncle's lap and patted his shoulder. I didn't expect his hand to grab me by the top of my pajamas.

He carried me by my collar like a policeman would do to a nasty criminal. He slammed my head against a faux-marble fireplace lining and I could feel the blood trailing down my neck and sticking in my hair. He brought his face down to my level once more as he sat me down.

He only said two words. 'Get out'

■■

Although we are immortal, pain still exists for us. Although we cannot bruise or bleed as individuals we have decided to bond in a human form.

Humans bleed.

We were components of a human, sealing the form of this little girl together as if we were her average skin cells, blood cells, and etcetera.

This is how we will spend eternity.

The role we play sometimes causes pain on a large scale. A single cut can sever through billions of us—trillions depending on how long or deep the course. Though we do heal very fast the pain is immense.

After all, we are not merely replaced in her body as cells would be after a wound, we remain, and clutch to our own magical properties. Each entity, each faerie experiences the pain separately. We can never die, so the memory of our pain will be permanent.

However, as a whole, we believe that any sacrifices will always be worth it, for Talib has been a dear and faithful friend.

55

Aside from that, curiosity is our creator in Husrodolg... humans secrete curiosity naturally.

Joslin's father had a spirit thriving on curiosity, and we form his "spitting image" spiritually. There is nothing Joslin doesn't wish to know—nothing she won't strive to investigate once her interest is taken.

Still, unable to predict the future, we "tharpels" as Talib calls us had no idea that evil within one mortal could grow to be so strong on Earth.

The very idea of such a truth was unfair.

This strange man... the one called "Owen"... he seemed so harmless...

■■■

I whimpered and struggled away and managed to get to my room crying and dragging my blanket with me.

When I tasted my blood in my mouth, you can only imagine how terrified I was. I must've bit my tongue in that instant, my whole head had been jolted and in my surprise, I was certainly unprepared.

I ran up to my chosen bedroom and to my bed and whimpered. Visions painted my mind like a frustrated artist's painting, a splash of red here and a swirl of colors over there. I eventually lost consciousness and when I woke up, Owen wasn't there.

I sat down in the hall and cried, my whole body pulsing with pain. I grimaced at the sight of the blood on my hands. It had dried, but it smelled awful. I didn't know blood had a smell, but it did, and it was putrid. I didn't know at all what to do except to cry for a while.

I walked to the end of the hall and opened up the door. It was a typical bathroom. Clean. Nice. Rather untouched. There was still one door, that fifth door, I hadn't opened, but at that moment I didn't want to. I ran to my suitcase in the first room and grabbed my toothbrush.

When I brushed my teeth, I shivered and my breathing stopped when I felt an ice-cold hand on my shoulder.

"Clumsy, aren't we?"

I frowned, looking at his reflection in the mirror, then at the side of my bruised and slightly cut head. Then he turned me around fiercely, dug his dirty nails into my shoulders and looked me eye-to-eye.

"Clumsy, aren't we?" he repeated.

I nodded, "Yessir."

"Call me your uncle."

I simply nodded.

Chapter 2: Family

Near to autumn, 2154...

When their journey ends, Miranda and Joslin both get out of the car quickly. Joslin feels like she's been trapped in that box for forever and finally has a moment of relief. She takes a deep, happy breath of muggy air in and sighs heavily; grinning as she taps her feet, crosses her arms and shivers.

Miranda squeaks as she runs out of the driver's side door, and over to the passenger side.

"Hey, Jossy, ya wanna help me with these boxes?" She asks, simpering.

*It's Joslin, Miran*da, she thinks, glowering, "Yeah, definitely," she says softly.

Miranda grabs Joslin's bag and her own bags and starts fumbling for the keys as they make their way toward the front door. Joslin lifts the three big boxes out of the passenger seat. They aren't too heavy, but not very light either.

Miranda doesn't get a hold of her keys for about six minutes, and she starts laughing, thinking: *Miranda, the boxes are slipping, what the Hell do you have in your purse that makes keys so hard to...*

"Found them!" Miranda shouts.

She unlocks the door and shuffles in with Joslin trudging behind her. Joslin sets the boxes down on the kitchen counter and huffs. She then tilts her head upward and smiles at a wall of boxes. The temporary barricade blocks their way from any other part of the house except for a small hallway and a closet door.

"So," She says.

Miranda jumps.

Joslin supposes that Miranda must be unused to her voice because she hadn't talked nearly the whole way to her house.

Joslin laughs, "Sorry, Hun, but where am I gonna stay?"

"Oh!" Miranda giggles, "Of course, I'm sorry, I was spacing off."

Joslin smirks and rolls her eyes.

Miranda opens the closet and for a moment in her head Joslin thinks she's made Miranda upset.

*"Well, if you're going to be **that** way—rolling your eyes at me, YOU can sleep IN THE CLOSET!"* Miranda yells at Joslin in her hypothetical thoughts.

She laughs at that idea and shakes her head when she sees the obnoxiously fuzzy winding stairs.

"Yeah," Miranda says, "I thought it was a closet too."

The shag-carpet spiral staircase leads into an incredibly interesting basement area. The walls on the left side are wooden, stained, and very expensive looking and to the right simply stone-brick walls have been lain with an extensive small gap near the floor.

As the two walk closer to get a better look at that wall, L.E.D. lights turn on to present little water fountains in the gaps. The lights switch color from red, to blue, to violet, to green, then yellow and continue.

"O-meh-God, that is super…" Miranda exclaims, walking over and crouching down to touch the water, only to have her hand run into a thick sheet of glass. "Cool!"

Miranda grins widely, her golden lipstick sparkles in the fluorescence. She turns her head to look at Joslin and grin even more, her dark skin dipping into dimples.

There are three doors, one on each wall, in that small section of the basement: one grey, one black, and on the back wall is an unpainted wooden door. The door on the back wall straight ahead of them seems to only lead to a storage space, and has no bulb to light the way inside, so the girls leave it be.

Joslin turns and opens the grey door, "Have you explored down here yet?"

"Nope! Joslin, remember, I was telling you in the car that I went down to Florida in the first place to find my old high school friend, Brittany.

I found you first." She smiles.

Joslin can tell that Miranda's thought should've just made her day, but the fact that Miranda thought of her in the first place meant absolutely nothing to Joslin. She just keeps her slight smile, her face unchanging.

They go through the grey door and venture momentarily into darkness. It feels safer than the other door because of the carpet beneath them, so they continue on until Miranda finds the pull-switch.

A room lights up. The beautiful designs of floral swirls plastered onto the walls captivate Miranda.

"Oh my god!" She says, smiling like a Cheshire cat, "They made this better than I could've even imagined!"

She traces her fingers along the patterns

She'd turns the light on to a room bigger than the one they just walked out of. She looks around and realizes it's a closet! There are racks, poles, hangers and shoe cubbyholes aligning every wall. Miranda makes high-pitched squeaks and does a little dance of happiness in the middle of the floor. She intently looks at just about every nook and cranny in the room.

Joslin walks over to the other end of the room, bored from watching Miranda's hyper-energetic stupor and gasps at a door hidden behind a half-wall, "Oh my Lord." she says, "I don't believe it...you have a closet in your closet!"

Miranda walks over, "Really?"

Joslin appears flabbergasted, but at the same time, she somehow recalls overhearing bits of Miranda's solo conversing during the long ride over. Although she hadn't been listening, she gathered some information.

Miranda had apparently told the builders a rough idea of how to construct the house and what she wanted. Obviously, they achieved a final product beyond her dreams.

Joslin realizes that evidently Miranda just saw everything today.

Miranda turns the knob and the "second closet" was actually just a small bathroom, but with a shower and tall candles.

What a strange construction pattern... Joslin thinks as she peeks into the restroom, and turns back to look through the closet to the other side that leads into the bedroom.

"Sheesh!" Miranda says, "Like, they furnished it for me a little."

"Uh... are those candles used...?" Joslin mumbles, wiggling her eyebrows.

"Hey," Miranda smirks, shrugging it off, "I guess the builders had a little fun on break." She nudges Joslin's shoulder.

All Joslin can think of is a fat, hairy construction worker in a romantically lit bath... She has to shake the image from her head to avoid an awkward conversation.

She blinks and spins herself around, "Okay time for the other door!"

They run over and find the same exact design, only on a different side.

Miranda beams, "So..."

Joslin looks over.

"Which room do you want?"

Joslin opens her mouth to say, "It doesn't matter" when Miranda shouts out, "I call grey!"

She laughs and Joslin chuckles a little, and then stifles herself with fatigue, "Eh, Miranda? I'm real tired, I'm just going to get out my sleeping bag and camp out in my room... if that's okay with you..."

She looks up to see Miranda's expression, and is relieved to see her oblivious still.

Miranda smiles and says, "Okay, Joslin. I'll be upstairs trying to figure out those boxes."

Miranda shuffles up the stairs, pauses, and returns, "Oh, and if you need me, open your door 'n holler, m'kay? The contractor said that these walls are sound proof."

Joslin nods, and in a flash, Miranda's gone. Joslin stands there for a moment or two. She isn't exactly free from the thoughts ranting inside of her head. If the rooms really are soundproof like Miranda said, then she's grateful because the rant pushed towards her lips, trying to become audible.

Joslin walks into the unclaimed room and makes it hers by setting out her sleeping bag and a little lamp from her duffle.

The lamp burns and when she gets up to flip the light switch off, shadows fill the empty spaces in the room. She lays down on her side, and concentrates, and finally manages to continue her thought-rant.

She's slowly leading up to some good memories and she doesn't want to go to sleep with the awful feeling of remembering the pain… but she can't skip through those memories either.

She only wants to rest, so she places the sacred journal down, closes her eyes and reminisces, talking to herself as if telling someone else a story…

"It's 2142

It's raining outside... What an amazing thought provoker...

Screaming each time droplets prod and prick its body, the puddle at the edge of my uncle's truck is rippling. It ferociously announces its pain, but accepts the abuse of the rain, for it has no other choice.

—this mirrors my position as a young child. The water screams without any sound just like I had. I always attempted to scream, but the pain intensified and my bewildered body wouldn't allow me the opportunity to express what I felt.

Once, Owen was drunk and I was in the kitchen and he took both of my arms and tied them to a chair with some rubber that he tore off of his truck door. Then he tied my legs together and grabbed another chair and beat every part of my body until my white skin was stained pink with the flow of my blood underneath. My eyes seemed out-of-socket as they watered tears down my face.

When he saw that he hit much harder and bruises turned into welts. I tried to put my involuntary actions (like crying) under control. I sat there for hours after he decided to leave me.

I healed. Miraculously, the next day I had absolutely no bruises at all.

So, he continued...

Another time, he took some barbed wire.

He grabbed one of my arms and tied it to the railing and sat there, watching me struggle. After a minute, he took the other arm and tied it to the front door knob. He left me there stretched out for about six hours while he went out getting wasted, and the more I struggled, the more the wire cut in.

I remember the feeling of the wire slowly opening my skin. Then Owen would come home. He opened the door, which yanked at the wire, sending spikes into my wrist. Then he would kick me. With that one kick in my back he broke the cable and sent me head first into the wall.

I felt so weak.

But again I healed, and the next day, my fast-rated healing scared me.

I knew at that moment Owen was trying to kill me because every day was a different day. No moment with him was the same as the last and in a strange way; I almost admired his creativity.

I got a slight thrill when I went to sleep at night along with horror, wondering which card he would play next, and how I could handle it.

I was trying to understand the way he thought before he made me bleed or bruise. It was sick, and I felt like I put myself to shame. Still, I couldn't help it, because maybe I'm a tad insane to think in such ways, but it seemed commendable.

He wasn't only hitting.

There were slow ways to hurt me. There were times where he took my arm gently in his hand and slowly gave me three deep cuts. They were completely in line with each other...

And when he watched me—when he stayed... the wounds wouldn't heal. My body hid its magic from him, but healed me after he had gone, but much too soon. It provoked suspicion, thereby provoking further incidents— ***worse*** *incidents.*

By the end of August though, I was able to venture into the backyard without second-guessing myself at the back porch. One day, I mustered up the courage and ran, letting my curiosity lead.

I felt my foot lift off of the black oak deck and onto the grayish-red dirt. My eyes strained not to look back and see if the wind was really Owen breathing down my neck.

I finally made it; I had made the great escape. I ran and ran until my breath was short and I had to sit down.

Catching my breath, I looked around in the clearing I found and my eyes landed at a willow tree near the stump of a black oak.

A gleam of moonlight flickered off of a silver hinge and at once I noticed the black oak tree-house in the middle of the willow. Dozens of spear shaped hoary leaves swiveled through the night air around the tree as I ran again to reach it.

I climbed the wooden planks leading up to the wooden infrastructure and that night I slept there. I slept with not a care in the world and watched happily as my wounds glowed to suture.

...I remembered in that moment talking to my mother once.

Just two years earlier, in 2140

I said, "Mommy?"

She smiled, "Yes, sweet angel?"

"You know when you get hurt and your wounds glow and then go away?"

I was still smiling, but Aina looked distraught after I spoke.

"When did you get hurt? Why don't you tell Mommy these things? That's not supposed to happen to you!"

Then Talib showed up, covered head-to-docker in dust from what I supposed was his day's work (and also thought perhaps it wasn't),

"Good afternoon, kiddo."

I nodded to my father, and then watched as he whispered something into Aina's ear.

My mother then turned to me, and crouching to my level, asked, "So what about this glowing healing? Do you want to talk about it?"

I nodded vivaciously, "I like it! Sometimes when I watch, it doesn't happen, but when I look away, I can see it from the corner of my eyes. I have a question, mommy."

"Yes, darling?"

"Am I a faerie too? Like you?"

Well Talib had already been chuckling a little, and Aina started laughing too at that point.

"Sweetheart," she told me, "You are your own person. I actually don't glow like you do."

"That's because your necklace takes your glow away." I said, smiling.

Aina was distressed once again. I had never experienced a moment when she didn't want to talk to me, and there it was.

Talib told me to sit there on the stairs, as they both went into our den and spoke softly.

"I can't talk to her about myself. I mean it's one thing if she finds out about **her**self... She's not supposed to figure things out this early," Aina said, "How is she ever

67

supposed to be a normal little girl?"

*"She never **will** be darling. This is the way she was born to us, and I wouldn't change it for the world." said Talib, "She's a brilliant stunning child. Now, we don't have to reveal anything for her, she'll discover things in her own time. You shouldn't get upset about that, Aina, my love."*

I had walked over to the edge of the den and was listening in when I heard Talib start to walk around. So, I quickly retreated back to my little sitting-step and waited.

Aina came back to talk to me, and Talib must've gone into the kitchen, or off again on another journey.

Aina simply told me to hide my healing, and once again she disregarded her own powers. She made it sound like I was the only one who could heal that way—that others would get jealous if I showed them a healing wound. The notion was simply silly in my mind.

*The next morning, I was the one distressed. I remembered how I gave my finger a prick once so that I could watch it glow. It would **never** heal in front of me. I felt like I had to trick myself, watching the glow from the corner of my eye...*

2142

Two years later, as I was laying down calmly in that tree house, the memory of my mother thinking that I was something special made me laugh a little, and smile while I slept. And that's what I needed at the time.

My healing had changed its ways since then. The morning after I fled from Owen, I thought about every time I'd been hurt by him in my head. My wounds would heal in front of me, but they also wouldn't heal if he didn't leave. It almost seemed that the more he watched them, the worse they'd get.

68

I wasn't used to bruises. If I had wounds before Owen got a hold of me, they usually healed before they could hurt. Now, it seemed my very skin was confused.

Speaking of confusion, I may have been a prodigy to life, or at the very least a fast learner, but I didn't know how to handle the situation I was in. I didn't even know how to feel about it. Whereas, I'd found an escape in the trees behind Owen's house, I couldn't help but want to go back to my room.

The black oak hut was not a home, but "the indoors" placed in me a sense of security. I'd spent nearly all my time indoors as a little girl with nothing to fear; nothing to run away from. Aina would take care of me.

I couldn't fully grasp that my mother was dead, and as for my father... Well, it just felt like he was on another trip. My parents were immortal, and so was I! Death could not confine us! Certainly not them...

And still, even though I was over 2000 miles away from my old home, I expected to be safe within walls. Yet, when I came back to the house I suffered greatly. Owen was waiting for me when I got there.

I had no idea that Owen checked to make sure I was sleeping in the house. I thought he hated me and had beaten me so that I'd leave. But he waited for me to return, just so he could hurt me. Just so he could be cruel, and disturb my poor growing mind.

How could I ever sleep there again? How could I not? I was so lost...

Owen scraped my spine with a steak knife. The cold metal, like a rock skipping across a pond, tapped my skin swiftly, making quick indents, and rippling pain, skinning me and then striking again. I had no choice but to scream.

I nearly passed out straight afterwards, but Owen taped my eyes open—yes, **taped** them open.

After a few moments of holding the knife to my last prominent vertebrae, Owen threw me to the floor, and released my wrists from his grasp.

"Don't try my patience, child, you know as well as I do that you belong here."

My voice failed my thoughts when my head screamed, "PROTEST!"

What did he know?

I am meant to have freedom! My body is meant to move freely! I'm meant to dance and laugh and love my parents!

Where were my parents?

Why was I there?

Why couldn't it just end?

When I blacked out, a heavy rain poured down to me, and then I awoke. I could smell the soaked earth and plants.

As I suspected, Owen wasn't there.

"I must stay awake until he checks up on me each night," I said to myself out loud in his absence, "but still, how am I to know that he doesn't double or even triple check?"

I got up, drowsily. I ignored the stinging feel of my dirty back lacerations, entranced by how different the outside world smelled.

Usually when it rained so hard in this place, the world smelled like sweat and slight mold. Today, the rain brought out a beautiful verdant smell. My green eyes were locked in, looking out at the distant trees.

-That wood behind the house was quite a remarkable place.

If there were people like my mother, people like faeries, I felt as if they should've lived there. I felt almost at home among those trees.

In the rainstorm I ran barefooted, ignoring the stickers and sharp items piercing my feet, and disregarding the soft white glow that trailed after me each time the twigs and twine scraped.

In that moment and every time I was alone since, I would run out the door. As soon as Owen was out of the house, so was I. I'd sit and I'd wait under the unfinished structure in that willow tree.

Some days I would climb the tree, and some days I practiced ballet beneath it. Some days I cowered and cried beneath it. Some days I laughed, and played with its leaves.

I would have found a way, eventually to build more to that tree-house, but I felt as if it should stay the way it was.

I'm not a big fan of change anymore; it's hard to even say that I ever was. When I thought of building onto the tree-house, I'd decided: change had changed (ironically) into a bad thing.

Anyway, I still hadn't looked in that mysterious room by the end of the hallway. I knew then that the one at the very end was a bathroom, (what I used to call the fourth room) but there was something keeping me from the fifth.

I'd walk to the end of the hall, turn toward the door, and host a debate with myself as I fiddled with the chain of my mother's necklace.

*My **curiosity** and my nervousness were at the*

71

same level, but with all that I'd been through so recently, the tension broke and nervousness won over every time. I still couldn't open that door, but it wasn't like that was the only thing on my mind...

In a quick recap: I became 5 by January 23rd, 2142. My parents died in April. Owen kept me for the summer of 2142. By the middle of September, he surprised me with a certain sentence.

It was a typical question to give any five-year-old: "You ready for yer first day of school?"

I was sitting on my wooden chair eating a sandwich in what Owen called a kitchen. I did a double take towards the doorway when he said those words.

"Joslin?"

I stood at the doorway to the living room, not daring to step a foot inside, as if the floor would chomp at my foot if I did. I looked up at the back of his easy chair, where his bald head peeked over at the top.

"I don't know—I guess I never really thought of it." I said.

That wasn't true. I could write you an essay on the folly of that little lie. I couldn't count the times I thought about school. Not only that, but dreamed of it every chance I could.

"Well, I suggest you start thinking about it, 'cuz yer going tomorrow."

I smiled with one of my biggest smiles.

The excitement of a new school was something Mother used to randomly rattle on about.

Thinking about how my parents dreamed of a moment like this slowly made my smile fade...

...I did not want Owen to be the one to take me to

school. That was a job for my wonderful mother.

I walked up the stairs with determination.

Some murderous heathen had killed my mother, I may have gotten distracted several times, but I'd never stopped thinking of her.

The most I learned from Owen was how to take care of myself, which I probably would have learned without help from him anyway. I mean, I learned to read at age two. I taught myself self-maintenance—it came easily.

The arts, creative spirit, happiness, and any other valuable parts of humanity—not necessary for survival, but necessary for a reason to live, those were things that my parents gave to me.

I did have reason to survive though, because there were always chances in every day of finding a reason to live. The greatest gift my parents gave me was curiosity.

I will never stop pushing my boundaries. I will never stop searching for interests and solutions.

So, I would walk myself to school, because I would not let Owen ever replace my parents. They had already taught me how to read and write as much as they could before they had to leave me.

I cleared the third room (the one that I nearly couldn't open) and found an old-fashioned dictionary, among several Steven King novels, and dozens of DVD's. The toys in the room were mostly under my age level.

There were too many teething toys, and absolutely no way for me to dispose of them without notice, so I stored them all in the ironically empty closet. I figured that would be an intensely cluttered area, but the only thing on the floor was a thick sheet of dust.

I speedily read through the dictionary, skipping through quite a few pages. I also read into the first chapter of a frankly disturbing novel called, "IT".

My basic point in explaining this endeavor is that obviously I didn't need to be in Kindergarten. The point of Kindergarten wasn't to learn or grow: school was an escape…

I got my clothes ready for the next day and went to sleep at eight-o-clock. I woke up at six-thirty so that I could ask for directions, and more importantly, avoid Owen.

I walked into streets that I had never seen.

*Every small whisper of wind reminded me of death. Of **their** death and my **fright**. I kept in mind that no matter what, my early morning walk would be well worth it.*

Tip Sod Town looked much different than anyplace in Iowa that I'd seen.

I believe that I lived in a more upper class area so even though I'm sure now that there are rinky-dink-near-to-ghost towns like Tip Sod in Iowa, I still hadn't seen any. (But of course, to be fair, I've never gone back to Iowa [even today, that truth rings true]).

*Everything was so **old**. It was slightly comforting, and also mysterious.*

All those words could describe my father as he lived. So, I smiled and warmth filled my chest and the flesh in my cheeks.

I looked both ways and then crossed the vacant highway, then skipped to a jagged sidewalk. All that was in sight for me besides my own two feet were trees and a gas station.

The sun was at its peak in the sky. It sat, a bright

pink bulb emitting from the edge of the earth. Around it were strips of wispy blue clouds that seemed to be in a slow dance that revolved around the glowing light of the sun. I followed them, dancing gracefully along the cement path.

I'm sure it looked odd to see a girl with so many bruises dancing so gracefully. I was more bruised than my mother and she was far clumsier than I! (The dark thought made me giggle.)

I reached the spot where the gas station was and hopped off of the sidewalk. I looked at the lines on the cement-top parking lot as I slipped toward the red-rimmed doors.

As I looked around the store at the merchandise, I thought about my bruises. I whispered my thoughts out loud.

The questions presented themselves suddenly, but as they did, they pried, "Why haven't I healed yet?

"I always heal. Has Owen done something to me? Perhaps it is the darkness of that house... does it yield the light of my healing? Does it destroy my abilities? I must find out..."

I stopped muttering my thoughts and attempted to peer over the counter. It stood way over my small head, even with me balancing on my tippy-toes.

A chubby, bulbous-looking woman sat in a chair behind the desk inside this building. Her blonde hair was tied in a bun with a pencil stuck in the middle. I heard her foot tapping and braced myself for talking. (I didn't really like talking so much anymore.)

I was about to ask her my question when she asked one first: "You lost, little girl?"

Then she looked up in an inquisitional stare,

glossy lips puckered and eyes wide.

When I didn't answer she looked at her long pink-painted fingernails, and said, "If you're lost go back to your daddy, I'm sure he'll getcha a present."

Then she spun around in her chair and read a newspaper. I rolled my eyes when she turned and walked around the cash counter and tapped her leg. I winced as she lifted her hand and put her newspaper on the counter.

Hands lifting in the air startled me slightly... for understandable reasons.

She sighed and knelt down, "What can I do ya fer, little miss?"

I smiled as sweetly as I could possibly smile for this fat, pompous lady and said, "Um, big miss, could you tell me where the kindergarten is?"

The words sounded extremely childish coming out of my mouth. I meant for them to sound that way and it paid off, but I felt like scrubbing my tongue off. Falsehoods are not becoming.

*Still I accomplished convenience; she was so eager to help that she **cooed** at me.*

"Oh, sweetie, it's your first day, huh? Well, keep walking the sidewalk straight on forward and you'll run into the diner. Stop in there and buy yourself a donut." She handed me a dollar bill, "And Ken, the cook will getcha to the school."

I stuffed the dollar in my pants' pocket and beamed up at her, "Thank ya, ma'am."

I started walking out and she hollered, "Oh, no problem, dolly."

I still don't remember what I did with that dollar, but I didn't spend it on a donut.

I pushed open the bell-ringing door and started walking down the jagged sidewalk that seemed to lead into the sun. Things seemed to dance a little less, now that I had talked to yet another irritating person.

I hopped forward onto each square that pulled ahead of me. I stopped when I got to a crossroads. The sidewalk kept going, just like the woman said, but there was a narrow red dirt road separating me from the rest of the sidewalk currently, and I saw a diner straight ahead from THAT path. It sat at least ten blocks away at the end of a large vacant lot, which every building in the town surrounded.

"Dumb lady..." I thought aloud, and then I broke into a run toward the diner.

*So, those directions weren't the best. I didn't really even **need** to stop into the gas station. I did perfectly fine on my own.*

A faded sign at the top corner bruised with rust said "Mlisbled Diner". I open the door that led inside. More bells tingled.

"Are they elves or something?" I thought to myself, "What are the bells for?"

I reached the first round table and sat there in a spinney chair watching the young boy that was staring at me from across the room.

He had a sort of strangeness about him that I appreciated. I mean he looked like any average child, except he was completely "ginger" (although I didn't know of that endearing term until much later).

He had freckles, reddish brown hair, and he was missing his two front teeth. He wasn't fat and wasn't skinny.

All of that, I'd noticed after I stared back at him.

Then I looked straight into his eyes and I'm not sure what, but there was something there. A spark of knowledge, maybe? A spark of intrigue, more likely, but whatever it was, I most certainly wanted to know.

Then I examined the rest of him in all of two seconds and realized that he was still staring at me, "What's with you?" I asked.

"What's it to ya?" he said back to me.

Those were all of the words that were passed between us when from within the kitchen someone shouted, "Eddy! If that's you, ya better get yer fat ass outta here or I'm 'a kick it the hell out myself, you drunken dirty bastard!"

The boy glared at the man's words, as they seemed to float by in the air. He walked toward me with his hands in his pockets. "I'm sure sorry that you had to hear that. I'm Justin." He said and he extended his hand to me.

I stared at it, "Well, what do you want me to do with that?"

Justin frowned at me, "Well, grab it, a 'course, dummy!" So I did and he shook both of our hands up and down rapidly.

And all the time I'd been alive before that moment, I thought that only older men with suitcases shook hands with each other. It seemed incredibly unorthodox and silly for us to do it.

When he let go the man who spoke before came out of the kitchen. He looked to be about in his forties with dark brown hair that seemed to be trying too hard to hide some greys.

He had a clean-shaven face and his eyes were a little droopy. His face was stern but it transformed into a soft, gentle one when he saw me, "Aw, little lady, I'm sorry if ya heard that. It's not right for such young little girls to hear such cussin'"

Justin scoffed.

Apparently, it was a stupid thing to do because the man glared at him. Justin didn't wince or even flinch; in fact, he stuck his tongue out at the man.

"So, I see you've met my hazard of a son here. Was he a gentleman to you?" He said, looking at me with sleepless eyes and drying his hands.

I nodded, "Justin welcomed me very kindly." I replied as sophisticatedly as possible.

He had a puzzled look for a moment then broke from it, "So what's yer name, young lady?"

"Joslin," I told him.

"Are you in Kindergarten just like Justin here?"

"Yessir."

"Well, okay, I'll let him show you the way; it's about time he's made a friend."

Justin stumbled toward the door and that was that. His father didn't say, "Goodbye, son, I'll miss ya!"

He said nothing more and Justin just left, with the sound of the ringing elf-bells on the top of the door. So I waited for a few minutes, puzzling, then I grabbed my duffle bag.

Owen didn't buy me any school supplies so I improvised. I searched through the stuff I'd organized before in the third room, and found what I figured would suffice.

Anyway, in the Diner Justin's father seemed to feel awkward just standing there twiddling his thumbs, so

I walked along to join Justin. His head was turned down and I could see a tear running down his cheek. I decided not to ask him about it.

Apparently boys don't like you to see them cry, though I can't remember where I heard that or why they were that way.

Then, all of a sudden, Justin busted out in a ranting word explosion. "He just don't care anymore! I can't see why! He's my dad, an' I love him, but he can't love me. And, 'mind ya it never was that way before my mom left us. She destroyed him! I hate her..."

He finished and I could practically feel the heat rising from his flesh.

I was familiar with the word "hate" from storybooks. I wasn't sure I'd ever felt that way about any human. Hating Owen might've been easy, but I just didn't. I didn't understand him enough to truly hate him. I suppose that back then; I was much too gentle and had no will to delve into hate's meaning.

Later on in my life I knew others who'd been abused and hated their abuser. I guess it wasn't fair in some respects that I healed so quickly nearly every time. I thusly had more time to be calm since I spent less time in pain. Perhaps hatred came from dwelling on those moments. I couldn't be sure.

I thought that Justin was being a bit unfair to his mother, but I didn't fully understand the situation, "It's not her fault if she died, you know." I said after my thoughts were collected and a tiny shock wore off.

"What?" He snapped in return to my soft remark, "No! She didn't die! She just left us! She stopped loving me 'fore dad did."

He sniffed, but his runny nose let loose a liquid

trail from his nostrils. He sniffed again, and it disappeared. I scrunched my nose up as he continued his nonsense-talk: "I guess he thought that if he followed suit she might come back." I blinked in disbelief as he looked at my reaction.

Then he concluded once more, "She ain't never comin' back." And with that said he looked down again.

"I don't believe you." I said.

He looked up with a frown, "Why not?"

"Because parents just don't stop loving their children like that... At least, not where I'm from..."

"Well where yer from sounds like a faerie tale ta me, sweetie."

I thought about my faerie mother and my pale vampire dad in the irony of what he just said. Then I replied, "No... Faerie tales have nice endings. Mine doesn't."

"What happens in the end, Cinderella?" he said, being sly for his kindergartener self.

I think he was expecting a giggle reaction, but I was too lost in my thoughts, "My parents died."

I looked at him, feeling my eyes turn to glass as I stared straight through him. I stated, "They were murdered."

His eyes grew wide and then he returned his gaze to the ground once more.

I saw him, but only in blurs. I wished that I could've stopped freaking him out so much. I hadn't even begun to make a first impression, but it wasn't like I was used to meeting new people anyway.

Besides, there was no use in me trying to be average in that moment. I was nearly frozen in eighty degree weather, as the scene of their death went through my mind over and over again without ceasing.

I nearly tripped on a part of the sidewalk jutting up from the ground, and the scene flashed away as I balanced. It took me until then to realize that Justin was looking at me and smiling.

"I think I like you Joslin... a lot"

I blinked a few times, "Well, er, uh, okay," I flushed and then thought, 'what is he talking about so irrelevantly? Of all the random things to say! I thought he'd ran off! I told him my parents were murdered and now he likes me? What does that even mean?'

Dissatisfied with my uneasy response, he added: "I mean I got yer back if you got mine."

"Deal?" he said.

I tilted my head to one side in confusion, then with a random burst of happiness (which I was not expecting) I said, "Sure, Justin, anytime."

With our new alliance already made... (From where? I didn't know; it made my head spin around just thinking about it.) We walked into the opened red brick building.

"Tip Sod Elementary", it said in brass letters along the side. The elementary school was connected to middle and high school, which I thought was pretty neat.

Justin led me into a room with several noisy children that were all around our age.

I shouted above the bustle, "Jeez Louise! What do they have to talk about that makes them this loud?"

Justin rolled his eyes, "Well, guys or girls?"

I said, "Both."

Justin looked at them all like they were pathetic, "Mainly the girls talk about the boys and princesses, and the guys talk about dead rodents and eating worms."

I slipped my tongue back and forth on my lips, "Mm, yummy." I said sarcastically.

He had a face of disgust plastered on. "Eww." He said.

"I was kidding you, Justin."

"Oh."

Owen had taught me plenty of sarcasm, in our months together saying things like, "Yeah, that's a clean kitchen," (followed with a swat to my back) or something like, "Go outside and watch what happens."

I suppose you could say I was an expert in sarcasm. Justin however was apparently not. He seemed sheltered, even though his father was obviously not the most conservative man.

I looked around the room, eventually putting my petite hands on my hips as I scanned for intelligent life forms (In the words of Buzz Light-year). I finally caught sight of a little boy with shaggy black hair and unfitting clothes sitting behind an easel alone.

I grabbed Justin's sweaty hand and pulled him forward.

"Where are we going?" He asked.

"To get another ally." And I felt the grin stretch across my face.

Before he could ask me what 'ally' meant, I think he found out for himself.

We both poked our heads over either side of the easel and smiled at the little boy.

"Uh... hey," he said.

He looked up so that his hair fell out of his face. His eyes were brownish gold and beautiful.

"Hello," I said, jumping out from behind the painting. Justin mimicked my movement.

He looked at Justin, face unchanged, then smiled at me, and said, "Hello."

He brought his hand out like Justin had before, "I'm Eric."

I sighed and turned my head toward Justin who had been glaring at Eric but smiled at me when I turned to him, "Am I going to have to get used to this old man hand shaking?"

Justin patted my bruised shoulder, "Yes, Joslin."

I winced a little, "I'm Joslin. In my family we always hugged, but I guess hand shaking is great as well."

Eric frowned at me, "Haven't you ever seen someone close to ya 'sides yer family?"

I shook my head, "Nope."

Eric smiled, "Well, I'd be glad to meet 'em!"

I could feel my eyes light up and then dim as my heart flew and crash-landed. "Well, er, I wish you could." I paused a little, "But they were killed." I said shrugging.

Eric's grin turned instantly to horror-struck paleness. I guess children my age weren't used to the morbid nature of my current life.

Hell... I wasn't used to it, and I'm still not.

After a while of looking down, he stretched his

arms out. Gratefully accepting a custom I knew, I slunk into his arms. He was so comforting and warm. In a moment, my father was home. Suddenly I was in Talib's arms and I didn't want to leave.

My arms pushed me out of his grasp without me knowing. My brain, I thought was lost in a vision of me being with my father. As if I was looking from behind myself, I saw the teacher come to the front of the room. I felt remorse for leaving that hug. I felt my heart screaming for it.

Yet, my five-year-old body was attempting to keep me focused and out of trouble, and apparently, the other children felt the same way... just a little later. The authority driven voice spoke over the rest of the little tones, which disappeared in a flash. I wiped my eyes and adjusted my shirt and stood between my sudden "best friends".

The voice spoke on with somewhat of an overly happy disposition. I couldn't explain the feeling then as I held my stomach confused, but I can explain it now.

Bad irony: My new teacher was old and very much at peace; I was young and tormented.

At that moment, without a reason, I hated that woman who called herself our teacher. I scoffed, thinking of another bit of irony: Although a lot of the kids seemed to be eager to learn from her, this woman wasn't even a teacher to me because she taught things that I already knew.

(And I can't even remember her name now.)

Nevertheless, I sat among the other students— among them and in between the only family I had. My family was sudden, and we hadn't talked much, but we were family; I could feel it.

When the day was over and I had reviewed the alphabet and numbers one through ten without need, Justin, Eric, and I were the first ones to run out.

The other seven students spent some extra time in the coat closet waiting for their parents to come and get them.

The difference between them and us was simply that. **Parents.** Theirs were genuinely **caring.** Our parents... or guardians **weren't.**

Linked arm-in-arm, with me in the middle, we ran awkwardly to the Diner. Justin explained to me, that although everything in Tip Sod Town had an official name, they always called it by the noun. I.E., Mlisbled Diner was "the Diner".

We managed our way to the back of the building after an interrogation from Ken, Justin's dad, as to how *my* day went mainly.

"Well, did y'all learn a lot?"

Justin and I were silent. I didn't want to insult anyone who actually was at a Kindergartener's level. Eric made me less nervous about my progress when he said, "Pfft, no."

"Well, Eric, I wasn't really talking to you, **slacker.**" Ken Mlisbled stated. He said the words without any jest, as if he were talking to an adult.

Eric rolled his eyes, and walked ahead of us, toward the kitchen.

"What did he mean by that?" I asked Justin softly, when Ken interrupted his response with:

"Joslin! What did you get done today? Make any new friends, learnt some countin'?"

"Well, sure to both of those I guess,"

This conversation with Ken was utterly useless to me, and it dragged on for maybe ten minutes.

Justin managed to inch away, as I was interrogated.

I scolded both of the boys when Mr. Mlisbled finally said, "Well, I'll let you alone now. Have a fun time playin' around," and left with a wink.

"Why in the world would you leave me, you horrible children?" I said.

*Eric busted out with laughter, "Well, **somebody** has a crush on you; we didn't want to get in the way of his chances!"*

Justin punched Eric in the arm with a very mediocre-child-punch, but Eric still chuckled.

After glaring at Eric for a moment, Justin turned to me and said, "He's just real polite to girls, we'll leave it at that."

I shrugged. I didn't care about Justin's father as long as he didn't try to hurt me. Though it would get really annoying if he started to waste a lot of my time, but I figured I could find a way to stop that from happening.

After Justin's father went to go run errands or something, Justin gave us a short tour of the housing part of the Diner.

"That's the kitchen door, I'm not allowed in there, but I've been in there and it's not that great anyways. This is my dad's room."

He opened the door on the left, the first one, and closed it right away. "I'm allowed in there, but it's not a pleasant place to be."

We walked further, "This is the bathroom," he gestured loosely to a dark room. We walked to the last door, "And this, this is my room."

I cooed in little "oo's" and "ah's" along the way through the hallway and applauded when we got to his room. Justin smiled at me and Eric rolled his eyes. When I looked at them, they suddenly both smiled with their eyes shifting.

...Somehow I felt a tension between them that at the time I didn't understand.

We were all family and they were my first friends. The least they could do is be happy with each other.

I was happy to be away from Owen still, so any "problem" seemed like a trivial itch in a day of bliss, so I just grinned at them constantly. All three of us sat on the floor and I asked them about life in Tip Sod.

Apparently, Justin and Eric were already best friends. I remember at some point, one of them used the phrase, "three's company", but truthfully, all I would've been was a third wheel.

The two took turns being a third wheel instead of having me feel like the new kid. I had the "fault" of being too likable at times... I was great at being interested **and** interesting.

When either boy wanted to do something the other one didn't, I was always "game" or "gung ho" for it. Most of the time, I'd find a way to include the third wheel.

Before I came along, Justin and Eric would just do mutually thrilling activities. They explored the woods, chased woodland creatures around, vandalized old buildings and went on "escape route adventures". They longed to be free of their lives, but never truly wanted to take the chance to leave. They were comfortable in their discontent.

Eric loved to talk in general, but his eyes really lit

up when he spoke of their adventures. He put great details and thrilling exaggerations into their past endeavors.

Justin allowed him, and, in fact, **presented** him as the story-teller. Eric had a far more expansive vocabulary than the two of us, but what's even more impressive is that at his age of seven back then, he already knew how to recognize his crowd and speak their language. No matter how he changed his words, the tales were enthralling.

I watched Justin's face while Eric spoke, which was probably rude to Eric, but I couldn't help it. Justin seemed to be entranced by his own visions of their now-spoken memories.

After several minutes of staring at his face without him noticing, I had to suppress the urge to ask Justin a question. I didn't want to interrupt Eric.

So, because I could think of nothing else to do in my **absolutely dire** situation, I did that stupid thing that we were taught to do in Kindergarten.

Two sets of eyebrows lifted as I raised my hand, so I giggled a little.

Eric halted his words, and paused with a humored expression on his face before he said, "Yes, Joslin?" in a very professionally-sounding adult-like fashion.

"Well... Err... I have a question for Justin..."

"Um, Okay...?" Eric said, sounding dejected.

"Shoot!" said Justin, who was now peering into my eyes excitedly with those sharp green interrogators.

"Well... I wanted you to tell me... your parents' story..."

I swear both boys became so silent that I could

hear the sound of chipmunks playing ten blocks away. Then the dishwasher in the kitchen started up its low buzzing noise, and I suppose Justin took that as a cue to speak.

"What does that have to do with anything we're talking about right now?"

It hadn't occurred to me, for some reason, until then that he might not want to share his past with me (this person that he'd just met). I swallowed a lump in my throat.

"Sorry..."

"No..." He glowered at me for a moment, and then looked down at the floor, frowning and blinking.

Then he looked back up, his eyes warm and glimmering, "You're not sorry. But that's okay, because if we're going to be friends, I'll have to talk about it anyways. Guess it's better to get it over with. I'm just gonna have to make you guys make a pact."

"Aye, aye!" Eric said, saluting brightly, trying to lighten the mood.

I felt my lip quiver a little, still shocked at how angry Justin appeared before, but I saw Justin smirk, so my lips lifted in reprieve.

"Joslin?"

"What is it?" I replied to Justin.

"If I'm going to tell mine, we all have to tell our little dark stories."

He smirked, "Detailed as we can."

Justin was the only one smiling for a second, but then I shook his hand without even thinking about it, and my other hand shook Eric's. Then the two of them exchanged a handshake.

We all said, "Deal!" in unison, which was pretty miraculous, so we all laughed.

Then after about three minutes, Justin had prepared himself for the dismal story of his vanishing mother (during all of which I was gripping at my mother's necklace chain.)

"A year ago, about," he said, "when I had been four for a while (I can't remember anything before this time, so I remember a lot a' details). I was jumpin' on the parking curbs in the edge of the lot, ya know, in fron' of the Diner? I think I was waiting for my mom to come home in the first place. Dad said before that she'd be there sometime that week, so I was out there a couple times before that day too.

Well, anyways, a car that I didn't recognize pulled up to the Diner lot, three parking spaces from where I was at the time.

The only cars I'd ever seen was my parents', Eddy the bartender's piece a' junk and Sheriff Shutter's

"Pfft. Sheriff." Eric said, rolling his eyes briefly as he half-smiled.

Justin continued, shaking his head, "Her car was just rusted up as any of 'em. She put a foot down out of the car, walked toward my dad's Diner. I ran up behind her after she went inside, so that I could peep in and see why she was there.

"Turned out she was lookin' for a job as a waitress, or cook, cuz we don't need no waitress... or somethin' else—real boring stuff to me, so I kept waiting outside. I played around with some rocks, dirt n' dust, and then suddenly, Mom's car pulled up.

"She parked right away and gave me a huge hug and kiss... and I wouldn've rubbed off that lipstick if I'dda

91

known..."

Justin rubbed his forehead with his fingertips, "Before I could say anything, she asked, 'Alright, honey, where's your pops? Where's my man?' and so I nodded toward the Diner.

"In a crazy turn of moods and events and whatever else, in all of five minutes, there was some screaming. Then there was some under-breath cursing. My dad ran out after my fuming mother in his boxer shorts.

"I keep trying to look for the reason she left. She didn't like my dad going around the house in his underpants because, well, it's a public Diner. But to leave us forever because he was underdressed is just crazy."

I remember the last part of the story, mainly because I remember that back then I didn't even know what boxer shorts were.

My parents were either careful with their flirtations, or else never had any "inappropriate" ones. (That is hard, now, to believe because they had such a happy and flirtatious relationship). My innocence was where a five-year-old girl's innocence should've been when it came to sexuality.

Everything else about real-life horrors or oddities, intricacies (if you will), I'm sure I was levels higher than I ought to have been with that score.

I never asked what boxer shorts were though. I just figured it was a silly pair of some kind of shorts. 'That couldn't have been a reason,' were my thoughts too. Of course, when I looked at Eric, he seemed to think otherwise.

Justin continued, "Mom shook her sad old head at me and drove away. Dad had already gone back inside.

"So, I waited in my room for a little while, and, well the day was turning dusk outside. I waited for something to happen, any news from dad... or for mom to come home...

"The sun finished its settling down and my dad busted out of his bedroom door, locked it behind him, and busted out his cigarettes, ran out the front-swinging doors and drove off like mom."

By this point in the story, my eyes were wide. I was about to ask what happened to the lady who wanted that job, when he started talking again. I kept quiet and listened intently.

"I thought I was alone," Justin spoke, "and I was so confused, when I heard some shuffling from within my dad's room.

"After the shuffling, the doorknob shook, and kept shaking and wiggling and for a moment, I was scared.

"Then, I remembered that teenage girl... from before. I came up to the door and unlocked it."

I had begun to nibble at my nails a little. Justin continued:

"There I was, in silence again. She didn't open that door... So I did.

I didn't know what she was thinkin' but her expression was not a good one. I guess I'd be a little mad too if my boss accidentally locked me in a room."

Eric was the only one who rolled his eyes at that. Eric was the only one in the room who **really** knew what was going on in the story, even though Justin lived it, and told it.

I was oblivious.

Although Eric was seven—two years older than Justin (and I), I believe Justin actually **did** know as much about the situation as Eric did, but just didn't want to admit it to himself.

Justin had witnessed the high school sweetheart tragedy that his parents went through, but also had witnessed either the aftermath of a rape or illegal (underage) adultery.

That's a bit traumatic, and I think I'd deny that it happened too. Especially if my father were the culprit. I shudder at **that** notion though, and it's ridiculousness.

Justin continued his story, "I said, 'Hello,' to the lady, but she just shoved past me. She seemed harsh, but still polite, with every action she made. She didn't talk.

"She went into the kitchen, and I shrugged my shoulders, thinking she'd gotten the job, maybe. I went to my room, because if I'dda gone in there after her, she could'a told on me.

"Still, after a bit, I couldn't take it anymore and I peeked into the kitchen door, but the lady left already... I think she took a few things with her too.

"Next morning was when I saw dad again. He told me that momma weren't never coming back, and that she obviously didn't love me enough to take me with."

"Did you ask him about the teenage lady?" I questioned.

Eric rolled his eyes again, "There's no need. We all know she wasn't really there for a job, the home-wrecker."

It was in that moment that—for the first time ever—I felt like a notion went completely over my head. I didn't like this feeling. I couldn't even brush the feeling off, when Justin brushed off Eric's comment all-together *so easily.*

"Hey!" Justin said, breaking from the funk of Eric's last comment, "It's Joslin's turn!"

Were we supposed to be excited? Eric smiled and they both looked at me in earnest. Where were their horrified reactions from earlier in the day when I needed them?

What did they expect me to say? "Oh goody, let's get started on my depressing life story, depressing at age five"? or "Yeah, I'm glad I'll get to go through watching my parents die again in my head! Fantastic."?

So, I stalled.

"Well," I said, "Aren't you just in the middle of your story? What's happened to you since then?"

"Awe, come on, Joslin, I'm awful at talking. 'Sides, Eric already told you 'bout our adventures together. All else I've been doing is teaching myself pian-uh and guitar."

"Oh... well okay then, how 'bout Eric goes before me, since I'm the new kid in town... Kind of..."

Eric shrugged, "... sounds fair to me. I'd like to say before I get started though that I'm supposed to be in second grade, but I'm glad for once for my grandpa's stupidity, putting me in kindergarten so that I could hang out with you two.

"He told me, like I remember it, 'Eric, your brains was knocked around a little as a smaller child, so we're gonna put ya back so you can give 'em a rest.' Completely undermined my intelligence, as does Justin's dad every day."

"Anyway, second grade is probably no fun, and nobody is even in that grade level this year in Tip Sod."

95

"Well, so I'm gonna make my story shorter... a little more brief, because it's a painful tale.

"Not to say anything about how you told yours," he said to Justin, "But dragging mine specifically out would be like asking for self-pity, which is absolutely **not** what I want.

"I didn't have a very good dad. But I guess I wasn't a very good son either. I tried to be good at anything I could be..."

"I didn't always live here." He said, "I lived in Mississippi 'til last year. We had a big house and lots of money. The only problem was me."

I frowned as he continued: Not warm, comforting Eric, *said my thoughts,* He could **never** be a problem.

"My dad used to tell me every day that it was my fault that mom died; she died giving birth to me and it was **my fault**. The only reason he kept me was because my mom wanted him to.

"He'd hit me every day and call me words I'm not comfortable saying in front of a lady," he winked at me, and watched Justin roll his eyes. I rolled mine too, but smiled and blushed simultaneously.

Then Eric snickered and continued, "It wasn't until he got **real** violent that my grandpa, who was visiting, overheard and saved me from being crushed by our sofa. I was sent by the government of the two states (Alabama and Mississippi) to live with him. He's the town sheriff. He's old and weird and I don't really like him.

"Besides that, he helped put my dad behind bars and all dad was doing was trying to silence a murderer like me."

I felt my mouth drop open throughout that last part of his story. I didn't know what to say. If he killed his mother, that's murder. If he didn't mean to what was that? Eric was not a murderer though and I was sure of it.

I leaned over, undid my crisscross-applesauce legs and repeated my thoughts aloud, "You are not a murderer," I said, hugging him.

"How do you figure?"

I let go and sat back, Indian style, again, smiling, "Because I've seen what murderers can do. You didn't mean to kill your mother."

He sighed, "I guess... but speaking of which, it's your turn now." I blinked for a moment. It wasn't fair that they told me their stories if I didn't tell mine.

So, I did.

I sighed, but I explained life with my parents and the day that I found them in perfect detail. Once I got closer to the present, I made sure to leave out most parts with Owen, remembering his words, "Clumsy, aren't we?" every time I thought about telling them about the abuse. Also, I didn't want to be sent away like Eric.

I finished with, "And here we all are right now, sitting in the same parentless boat," I raised an eyebrow, "Isn't life great?"

The only response to give was a shrug, I suppose, because that's all I got. It was as if they were saying, "Eh, we're content, it's not that bad..."

I smiled. I felt the inspiring will to "truck along". To keep fighting the outcome Owen was trying for and to keep living, exploring, escaping, and now loving these boys. And that thought was certainly a good reason to be happy and proud.

We each climbed out of Justin's window, one at a time. They taught me how to climb out and back into the window without scraping myself. It took me a few tries, but when I had the little technique down, we ran down the side walk, behind the Diner, and in front of the school.

Earlier that day we took the turn into the schoolyard, but at the time, we were going the opposite way, more toward the highway than the wilderness.

Tip Sod Town was next to a strange highway. One which wasn't marked as a dead end road, but in the dusty distance it was, in fact, blocked by an expansive Alabaman wood that stretched as far as the eye could see.

Once I became more educated in poetry (which happened upon meeting Miranda) I called the dead end highway, "The Road Less Traveled". It shouldn't have even been recognized as a highway, and it certainly wasn't on "the map".

G.P.S. systems weren't even programmed to recognize the area...

Anyway, back to our small journey: it led us to a housing area that I had seen earlier when I came in on the dirt road. Every house was a single story and had curved chips of crumbling, cheap paint.

The first house, of what looked to be ten houses (two rows of five, I believe), was a quaint little place surrounded by cats.

"Ugh." I said, "Who would own that many cats?"

I looked onto the porch and saw an elderly woman sitting in an old birch wood chair doing something that looked like the knitting my mother did before from time to time (but not very often).

Now, before I go on with my story, I'll remark that smoking is (and had been since about 2115) illegal in several states, including Nebraska, Iowa (where I was from), Wisconsin, and Kentucky and a few others, I *believe.*

Anyway, the point I'm getting to is that I'd read no books about it, I never heard of cigarettes. Even in Justin's story didn't know what the Hell he was talking about when he mentioned his father owning them. At that point and time, I also hadn't seen "Dumbo" yet (a timeless children's classic...) and what I saw happening in the yard, to the woman with all the cats was totally new to me.

Horror struck when smoke started emitting from her mouth, "Oh my God! She's on fire! We have to save her!" I screamed, making her look straight at me.

I didn't understand why she wasn't screaming, or why Eric and Justin both decided to bust out in laughter all of a sudden.

"Come on, let's go!"

I started climbing the fence. They both stopped laughing and in unison screamed, "No! Joslin!"

I was appalled, "You two act as though you have no consideration for living things! That woman is in mortal danger! She needs our help!"

Disregarding my urgency, they started laughing hysterically again. This time I got down from the fence and punched them both in their guts.

Justin was first to speak up. They were both still laughing, but also rolling around with the pain of my pretty-good-for-a-five-year-old punch, "Joslin, that's called pipe smoke, the lady does tobacco." I looked at him still expecting some clarification.

Justin tried his best after three more minutes of contemplation a-midst his laughter, but Eric interrupted his attempt to speak.

"It's like air, only it 'smells bad and tastes worse,'

like my grandpa says. Old lady Tontines has to have it all the time, ever since she started the stuff like seventy years ago."

Justin said after him, "So she's not on fire."

With that, they both busted out in side-splitting laughter again. I squinted at them angrily, for it was all that I could do with the mixed emotions I had.

On the one hand, they were completely disrespecting me, questioning my intelligence and making snide murmurs that I couldn't understand the words to.

"Hey! I could punch those noses just clean off your faces!" I said, wiggling a fist.

After a few more hiccups and chopped-up chortling, they became silent. I wouldn't have actually punched them in their faces—I didn't have it in me—but it was funny to see my little threat work on them. My ego was no longer bruised.

There must've been some unspoken consensus between us three, because after their light-headed giggling, without a word, we all headed back toward the Diner.

"Hey! Let's go to my house, guys!" Eric said.

He seemed excited despite his apparent distaste for his grandpa earlier.

We had made our way out of the small neighborhood, and had the Diner in view. Eric seemed over-zealous now and had a skip in his step. He became kind of goofy when he studied the sunset in the sky.

In fact, he started to yell and hop around, as if there were hopscotch boards on the sidewalk, and this is what he yelled:

"Red sky at morning, sailors take warning, red sky

at night, sailor's delight..."

Then he started singing, "Yo, ho, yo, ho!

We'll have a delight tonight!

For pirates are we,

and we have just seen

a brilliant red sky here tonight,

har, har!"

As he inched ahead of us with his energetic movements, Justin and I laughed, and Justin told him that the rhyme was pretty cool.

The further Eric got past the Diner, the closer Justin and I came to passing it in the first place. We were just taking our time.

Also, the farther away Eric got from us, the closer Justin got to me. I didn't feel too strange about it until our shoulders brushed a couple times. So, I nudged him a little bit, and he nudged me back.

We were both looking at the ground as we continued to shuffle toward the direction Eric was going. Up until this point, I believed Eric was the shyer of the two, but it became pretty obvious that Justin had some major issues communicating things to people.

Slowly, but surely, Justin leaned his head over to whisper to me.

He said, "Hey."

*It seemed like he exerted **too much** energy just to spout off that little word.*

So, I said, "Hey," back, wondering where exactly he planned to go with this conversation.

We walked a little faster as the conversation

progressed, "Wanna play a board game later at my place?"

In other places, people had incredible technology. Places like California, and New York, rebelled against the presidency of 2125, just a little while before I was born. During the last year of her term in office, President Penny Mclaiden "went crazy".

She acted like a drunken royal, so they say, and she tried banning technology altogether.

There were groups of educated activists in her favor who would purposefully destroy means of technology in certain places.

On a positive note, instead of an iron fist (as it's said in the common expression), people said she ruled with a green thumb. She's actually probably the reason that the highway's cut off near Tip Sod.

Yet, the partly-Amish president didn't understand that most technology promoted a greener earth.

Of course, most people didn't go for the banning of technology, and all the politicians laughed at her for even saying that she wanted to ban it. In fact, they probably kept her in office as long as they had simply to laugh at her.

The technology of the world had come to a point where if you wanted to lose weight, you could click a button and lose it. Virtual reality existed on a higher level where one could actually put their physical body in a state of dormancy as if it were frozen and walk into a world that another human created. Then they could live there for hundreds of years, if they wished.

Many states were too poor to afford technology like this, so Mclaiden wanted to ban it, saying that "God didn't intend for humans to live so unequally".

*Before she could succeed (if it were even possible), her term ended and she of course was **not** reelected.*

I had heard of technological places. I lived in one of the rich states myself. Like in most of the United States, and most of the rest of the world though, Alabama was behind all of this progress.

Alabama, actually, was worse than most places. Along with many of the other southeastern states, they actually seemed to have moved backwards in time to the late 1900's.

Of course, I hadn't noticed any of this. While children in Iowa were playing with floating computers and Apple-Microsoft products, living on Facebook, and learning from technology, I was already smarter than all of them.

I was smarter, even though my parents' lives could probably have been compared to people from the 1800's.

*Tip Sod Town was a technological step **up** from the life I'd been used to. Traveling to any state from any other state was like traveling backward or forward in time. And leaving **my** house to go to, say, a park in Iowa, would've been like a leap 300 years into the future each time.*

Interestingly enough, my parents sheltered me from the technology. I'm to this day, unsure why, but almost glad for it, because although I missed out, I would've gotten bored more easily with Justin and Eric, I feel. Then again, if they'd accepted the technology of the day, maybe something could've prevented the murder...

*I ran through some thoughts and smiled brightly at Justin. "I'd love to play a board game, but I'll have to see if I'm... **let out** to do so..."*

103

Justin then proceeded to look me up and down, which was pretty creepy, and before I could ask him what he was looking at, he said, "So, you're pretty klutzy, aren't ya?"

"Excuse me?" I said.

I snorted thinking of my dad, making fun of my mother by calling her "klutzy".

"Well," he said, "Nothin' personal. Just askin' 'cuz I'm curious. Those bruises and scratches look like you've been doing some exploring of your own this summer, and yer either really klutzy or just not careful."

I looked at him, and I probably seemed a bit befuddled, but only because I was. I still wasn't sure why the bruises weren't gone already. Mostly, though, I was confused as to how he could be so dumb.

Obviously, it looked more like I'd been bludgeoned, but he was innocently oblivious.

He grinned stupidly, and even though he was absolutely wrong, and the truth was absolutely horrid, I couldn't help but grin right back.

I noticed that we had a silence looming over us after a while. It had been my turn to speak for too long, and gradually we both started to look toward the ground again.

"Well, actually," I started, "I'm quite graceful. I used to..."

I realized that bragging about my gracefulness wouldn't help me in this situation. I had to lie.

"I guess I'd like to think that anyways... I can get pretty darn klutzy when I'm out playing..."

"Yeah..." Justin said, "Well, ya know, me too. It's nothin' to be 'shamed of. Lots and lots of kids our age stumble 'round. I know I've never had perfect balance or nothin'..."

My pride was beaten down, and the wound had my heart pulsing firmly. I wanted to protest against my lies more than anything, but facts were facts.

The fact **was** that there was no better excuse for my bruises than the truth, but when I'd seen their faces after I explained my parents' murder, I realized that their worry wasn't worth the exposure.

So the second best excuse—even being the stupid lie that it was—it would have to do.

After Justin said his piece, we were each holding onto the silence once more, but this time I'd adorned it with beautiful thoughts and observations.

No more words about life and trials.

The scent of pine around us was near to intoxicating. I adored every moment, watching specks of red dust and broken cotton seeds fall as softly and slowly as snowflakes.

Suddenly, Eric shouted, "HEY! We're here!"

Justin and I were at least six blocks behind him. So we both grinned.

"...**I'm** here..." He laughed.

Justin and I both snorted and started racing toward the ivy-covered brick building. We walked through a rounded doorway, looking up at the top edge, which stood six feet above our heads.

A narrow unlit brick hallway led us to a place where the town appeared to be completely and utterly gone.

In our view were just four brick walls: two covered in ivy, one behind us with the doorway, and one straight *ahead of us with a metal fence blocking our way from what looked to be a misplaced front door to a house. The field beneath our feet flourished with weeds and grasses, the smell was somewhat moldy. Yet still, there was a mystifying effect.*

"Every time we go to your house, I feel like I'm breaking into a prison." Justin said to Eric.

"Well, it's in the back of a jailhouse..." Eric replied.

"Naw, that ain't why. It's the fence." Justin said as he started climbing.

Eric and I climbed after him and we all landed on the ground and coughed a little as some dust flew up from underneath the grass, which grew more sparsely behind the fence. Eric reached into a vacant space in the wall where a brick should have been and grabbed a key to the door.

"Okay... this is my house," Eric said as he opened the door. Once he opened it, the anticipation of our little journey had ended, and any mystifying feelings disappeared with the sounds of championship boxing and an old man cursing and cheering at a T.V.

I met Eric's grandpa and we shook hands. Shaking hands still felt weird. Sr. Shutter talked to me something about wearing seatbelts. It was kind of funny considering that no one in this one-horse town owned a car except my uncle, but he never took me on trips.

I laughed at the fact that the town had no deputy sheriff or any police force or fire department. I knew of those things, and their importance in any community.

I asked him, "How many policemen work for your grandpa?"

"What are those?" Eric replied.

"You don't know what policemen are?"

So, I explained to both Eric (and Justin who was equally oblivious): "Policemen are the fellows who hold up the law in a city... or town. They work for a chief, or sheriff and they bring criminals to justice, uphold traffic laws, and have coffee breaks.

"They are good people to have around. My dad had a picture of him and one of them shaking hands; he explained it all to me... I guess they were good friends, well acquainted... or something."

I smiled. At the moment, the memory felt like a little treasure that I'd uncovered.

"Okay," Eric spouted, "so policemen actually make sure you **don't** break laws?

"Hah, Joslin, I don't really believe anybody can truly uphold to what's good.

"Policemen? No. All we have is my stupid grandpa. He's too laid back and he hardly ever leaves the house except to go to the Diner and have a chat with Justin's dad or grab a beer with Eddy, the bartender.

"If he sees someone grabbing something from the Diner, he won't even do or say anything about it. He tells me what I can and can't do, and I can still get away with pretty much anything. He's a big fat hypocrite, that's what he is."

"Wait... you steal things?" I asked.

But I wasn't going to question him further. I thought it best to follow the ways of my new family.

If Cain Shutter was an irresponsible influence to Eric, he was as well to me. Justin also told me later that Eric stole things constantly, but he wouldn't ever admit to it. His philosophy was that anything in the town belonged to everyone. "Stealing" apparently didn't exist to him—at least not in town because the town to him was an *anarchy that people weakly attempted to tame every once in a while.*

Eric tore me from my thoughts, and stopped Justin mid-sentence.

He said, "So... yeah. Anyways, Joslin, you wanna show us your room?"

I didn't know what to say. I gripped my necklace nervously again. It comforted me, but I was still nervous.

I couldn't bring them into that house!

What if Owen went insane?

What if once they went into the door Owen slammed their heads into the walls?

*What **then**? My entire family would be gone in a matter of seconds!*

I tumbled through my mind to come up with a lie, a white lie, maybe. I was so sick and tired of lying to these boys though. Eric's eyes had a way of burying themselves into yours and Justin's face was just adorable.

"Um, I, I can't, I have to do..." I paused, "Anyway, I love you both, and I will see you tomorrow."

And so I hugged them, kissed their cheeks, and I ran, leaving them confused.

I only looked back once to see Justin scratch his ginger head and Eric say, "That was weird," and laugh with his eyebrows furrowed.

I giggled a little and continued to run.

*But I **didn't** see them the next day...*

...I ran as fast as I could.

As I've said before, I have an exceptionally handy memory. I remembered the exact route backwards to the gas station and then to Owen's decrepit home.

I tapped on the black oak door. It creaked open. It was as if the house itself had to groan. What scared me the most was that the door was unlocked.

Then I shrugged the fear away, "I guess that people like Owen don't have to worry about locking their doors at 7 o'clock in the evening."

My parents had always kept our front door locked, even when no one was inside of our house, just to rid it of evil or something to that extent (to keep the bad guys away).

I tiptoed into the hallway that he called a kitchen and fumbled through the food because I was sure that I was literally starving.

*When I **had** a loving mother, I ate breakfast each morning and ate every meal given to me: four meals a day, seven days a week. Then, in Owen's house, I was on my own. No French toast with peanut butter on it, no roast beef with potatoes, and if I wanted a decent meal there, I learned later that it was better if I just went to the Diner.*

I opened the refrigerator and felt the cool air seep out from the top. I stopped skimming around the food and looked at the temperature, as it grew colder. Mostly I felt the cold around my neck... Did cold air normally tighten around your neck like that?

I felt like my own supply of oxygen was leaving me. I put my hands up to my neck—anything to stop that air from leaving, maybe settle myself.

That's when I felt his hands. His ice-cold hands slowly took the life out of me.

I was shocked; I was usually prepared when Owen came because his entire body smelled of liquor.

He was sober.

If I were able to breathe, able to move, I would use all the life that I had to get away from his grip on my neck. I couldn't feel the floor beneath my feet; I couldn't feel my heart slow its beat.

I felt digging, crushing, and tearing of my neck. I tried to gasp; I tried to breathe.

I failed. It was worse to feel the failure than to know I was going to die.

Everything was over.

Chapter 3: Strangers and Time

Tepidly, the black cloud's anticipated rain blurred my view through the window to what I called the backwoods...

"Backwoods" translates to the hick-ass places in the US usually, but to me as a five-year-old; it meant the woods in our backyard.

We technically didn't have a backyard; the trees took up most of the ground space right at the end of the porch. That image was just a taunting glimpse of freedom and merciful relief.

I woke up on my bed with the plastic roses scattered around me: the ones I had placed on the windowsill before. The ones that used to lie on the floor...

I was holding one of them in my hands to my chest like Snow White did when she was dead and waiting for her life-kiss or whatever.

The month on the brand new calendar that now hung on my wall stated, "October" in bold font. Previously, I'd known we were in the middle of September (the start of the school year).

I winced as I got up.

Normally someone's first neck-ache, as I've heard, is in the bone or muscle. Mine was on my skin. It was like the skin didn't exist; but instead, some soft bruised rubber. I moaned as I walked to the bathroom to examine myself.

I was disturbed to find that I was in the same clothes as before. I know it's weird, but I was more disturbed with that than the black and blue skin marked with red scars under my head.

After all, I was unconscious for a long time,

wasn't I? How filthy I must've been!

I took a cold shower. I started the water up hot so that I could get cleaner, and then cursed. I thought I must've been on fire. I avoided touching my neck during and when I got out and put myself in a towel.

I did wonder, "Why haven't I healed yet?" aloud... I shouted those words, frowning at my pulsating veins underneath the raw skin.

I opened the door and Owen's unapologetic face looked at me suspiciously right as he peered into the threshold.

"I'm very clumsy, Uncle Owen." I said that with such a snappy attitude that made me realize just how much anger I was holding back from him.

I was only five years old for God's sakes!

He turned in my direction as I walked from the bathroom to my room. Before I could close my door for privacy, he was there in front of me.

"Excuse me," I said, "I'm getting changed."

He chuckled, "You're not going out in public until that particular bruise is gone,"

*I suddenly felt as though a switch of self-control in my brain snapped into an unruly position, "I don't **think** so." I said,*

"I shouldn't suffer any further for what you did. So you can kill me if you want, but if you don't and you don't let me go to school, I'll sneak out again, I know my consequences."

Although I was so young, I felt more mature than him and although I was weaker than I'd ever been before, I was able to stand up to him. Thus, I felt like I was carrying my world.

I felt so strong! So empowered!

Unfortunately, and much to my disappointment, his face was unmoved by my outburst, "I thought you might've felt that way, so I bought you this."

He threw me a zip-up hoodie. It was the first and only present he'd given me, and as he handed it to me, his voice had changed as if he actually enjoyed giving me a little gift.

I smirked, "Okay, Owen, but don't expect me to thank you."

He laughed heartily, like Old Saint Nick, except of course the laughter had a baleful air to it. I never understood why he wouldn't take me up on my suicidal offer, but the fact just made me feel even more empowered.

▪▪▪

Joslin continues to think about the parts of that incident that she can remember. She has no job to occupy her day, and no need of one with the comforts that Miranda provides her with. She doesn't **feel** comfortable though, in a town where she'd been held captive by her own innocence and fear; where she survived through a small version of Hell. It seems impossible to feel comfort.

She thinks about the absurd phenomenon that she'd been through. She knows in her heart—for a fact that any other child wouldn't have lived through those last incidents with Owen. Feeling the old scars on her neck, her brow furrows, eyes narrow, and she cocks her head to the side.

"A five-year-old... With my jugular scarred... I vaguely—in some strange part of my brain—I had a memory of 6th degree burns. It reminded me of the skeleton man story that my father read to me:

113

"All around my neck, my skin and muscle tissue were non-existent. The aortic vein had been broken. All of my cervical vertebrae bones were charred, from the atlas to the clavicle... Then after I'd passed out, slept for days, and woke up, the wounds healed enough to be classified as mere third degree burns.

"Now, if I consider that memory to be a mere invention in my head, it still makes no sense. Third degree burns left untreated are absolutely fatal. Also, I had no food or water for a number of days... it makes no sense.

"I healed slower than I usually do, but I shouldn't have even healed at all, my muscles within months stopped being sore. I should've died."

She becomes spooked with the notion, unsure of whether she considered it a miracle or a spiteful demonic godsend leading her to her current state. She appreciated the fact that she was alive. Living was certainly a good thing, but in Tip Sod?

Joslin only justified her choice to return with her lack of closure. She wasn't hiding from Owen (long ago it became apparent that he couldn't kill her if he tried) she was waiting for a good time to ask Miranda about her old friends and family...

She settles, resting her chin on her palms. *I am much stronger now,* She thinks, comically shining her fingernails on her shirt, *I've grown, and if I survived such an assault back then, I can survive any...*

Miranda runs into the kitchen, kisses Joslin on the forehead, and grabs her car keys.

"You okay, sweet pea?" She asks.

"Yeah, just thinking, reminiscing, you know."

"A'ight well, Imma run—I've got a *date!*" She squeals on the last part of the sentence.

Joslin rolls her eyes, "What, and you're excited? Like it's ever been hard for you to get a guy."

"Well. This one is a *real* find." She smirks, puffing her lips out, her eyelashes batting, "I haven't had a *one* like **this** boy."

Joslin smiles lightly, enjoying the excitement over what she sees as nothing (but was a huge deal, obviously, for Miranda), "Well, you'll have to let me know how it goes."

"Yeah, sure thing!"

And with those small words, Miranda flies out the door, cornrows and all.

So long ago I let a miracle go as if it were a passing word, or a puff of wind. As if hardly anything had happened. The near death experience surprised me, but I couldn't keep my sanity if I didn't write it off.

I felt more confidence from that moment though, that was for sure. Ever since that moment, until the summer before 2nd grade, Owen made frightening, but empty threats to mutilate, endanger, or kill me.

I thought to myself, "Because I stood up to him, he resisted. If I'd only known before-hand."

I hadn't even been awake for those cuts and the burns. It angered me that Owen not only took away my comfort, but he had taken away a natural right I had as a human: to remember.

I should have the choice to be able to keep

memories or to discard them. And I can't even mention how much it scared me to know that Owen just purely enjoyed the tearing of my very flesh regardless of my reaction.

I had made a decision: Owen was the Devil—a hilarious notion to place a bald, beer-bellied man in, but it fit to his character none-the-less.

If in the Bible, the Devil could come up in the form of a serpent, then there was nothing stopping him from taking on a human form. With that notion, I left the house, a bit more satisfied with myself, considering how I defeated the Devil and all that.

Right when I came up to the empty highway, I'm not kidding—out of the blue I saw a wild, looks-an-awful-lot-like-Tarzan boy running into town.

'That's unusual' said my face...

*This happenstance had been neglected in my vast collection of memories, and **even though** the moment was filled with stress, the memory of the boy **himself** was one of friendship.*

The innocent little love we shared from the time we met was so calming and true that the emotions were well-preserved remnants. They never decayed with the erosion of time, even when memory had been left unpreserved.

Christian was nine and I was five.

I remember him running.

His hair bounced down by his elbows as he ran shirtless through the trees behind the convenient store. I couldn't help but think of Tarzan. He looked just like the monkey boy.

*His skin was **so** filthy. Mud covered his bare feet so that they looked more like misshapen brown shoes. His* *hair looked as though without the mud clumps it would be smooth. Ash, soot, and burn marks covered him from head to toe. His breath was ragged and could be heard even from my distance across the highway.*

So, I stopped my "seize-the-day", tough-ass stroll, and broke into a worried run across the street, listening to his panting and the whimpering.

As soon as I gathered control from the run, and caught my breath, I tripped over my own two feet (let the record show, it was clumsy, i.e.: out of character). I did regain my balance with my average grace and confidence, and let my untimely composure delay me. I ran further, determined to catch up as the boy continued onward.

Suddenly to my body's relief and my mind's ultimate horror, the boy coughed and fell with a thud onto the concrete sidewalk outside of "the Bar".

Flailing my arms around neurotically, I continued to run to him. My baggage and odd outerwear made me slower than usual, but I made it to him before he passed out.

"Christian" he said, his eyes rolling back in his head.

Panting, he closed his eyelids hard, and choked a bit on his own spit, "And... our names..." his breath calmed, and he whispered, "Our parents... our parents are dead..."

His head rested on the palm of my hand and his breath became inaudible. So, I put my ear to his chest.

His heartbeat pounded in my ear, strong and steady. Although I knew the situation was dire, I became bored after a while, so I tapped my fingers on my head to the rhythm of the lovely beat of his heart.

"Our parents?!" I whispered, fast and excitedly, "**our**...?"

Christian's mud-clotted hair was the cleanest part on his body that I could see. It was drenched and he literally smelled like a swamp.

My pupils floated to the corner of my eye, peering at the light seeping through the branches of the cotton trees, eradicating my sight and creating false blue figures in my vision.

I was probably twenty minutes late for school, but I didn't care.

Eric and Justin were family and I missed them dearly, but Christian had captured my interest. And of course I couldn't leave him in the state he was in.

I was convinced that he was my older brother and it raised some more of that buried hope in me.

I brushed some of the old dried mud's ashes from the corner of his eye. They sprinkled from my fingertips down to the pavement and blew away in the harsh autumn's morning wind.

Still lying on his chest, I realized that I couldn't lie like that with him forever. I didn't want to leave his side, but there were no adults in sight. I would've yelled for help, but the bar was the closest place to where we were and I could hear the blaring music from outside. There was no one to call.

My predicament didn't change, and I was frozen with worry tattooed on my face. It must've been thirty minutes that passed when suddenly the outer bar doors swung wide open and Sheriff Cain Shutter fell to his hands and knees on the pavement.

He laughed and laughed in his drunken stupor as the bartender, Eddie, yelled at him.

I didn't listen to their conversation at all. I had to interrupt it right away, and I knew I wasn't interrupting anything important.

"Excuse me!" I yelled.

The conversation continued as if I'd said nothing, so I converted my yell into a shrill scream that made me feel as if my throat were on fire, "Excuse me!"

Eddie's eyes glazed over and he was once again the emotionless boulder of a man that I remembered from a brief encounter before.

"I NEED HELP," I yelled.

Finally, Eddie saw us, and Cain Shutter just stumbled away, blind to just about everything, still laughing and spitting.

"Holy God, what the Hell happened here?!" he said, his eyes widening as he walked towards us. He lifted Christian up by his armpits, and then threw him over a muscly shoulder, just like a sandbag in the winter.

"I think he was running from something..." I stated, trailing off in my very normal quiet voice when I started saying, "... and I think he's my brother..."

As I followed Eddie up the stairs, behind the bar, I looked around at the antiques on the wall.

They (whosoever "they" were) had many old looking props and posters of characters and objects that I was unfamiliar with.

I did recognize ships, because I'd seen pictures of them in storybooks, and a cartoon version in "The Little Mermaid".

This ship that I saw on the wall had three bears in it though, and the top of the poster said, "Winkin, Blinkin, and Nod" and I was absolutely unfamiliar with those three souls, but I was sure that the poster was an insult to their characters.

The fine-illustrated teddy bears had lazy eyes, crooked mouths, awkward stances, and Jack Daniels bottles in their hands. One was laying down, pouring the drink straight into his mouth, another was swinging on the mast with his free hand, and the third was drooling and chaotically trying to steer the ship.

I looked down from the picture. The stairs leading out of the bar and into where Eddie lived were made of wood, but they were covered in foil wrap, stapled to the edges.

God knows why.

Christian's ear, I noticed, was bleeding a little from the inside. I started to worry again and paid less attention to my surroundings.

Eddie moved fast through the rickety hallway upstairs, turned, and laid Christian down on the bed in his room.

He cleaned his wounds and a lot of the dirt with a damp cloth and peroxide.

He made sure to eyeball me a couple of times, as if to ask what the Hell I was still doing in his house... or the Bar or whatever it was now on this floor.

I knew that he had sympathy for me, though. He could tell that I was very worried and scared, so I took advantage of his silence for as long as I could.

Eventually he had to leave the room to get something, and I allowed myself the privilege to cry a little and relieve myself of some strain.

When he returned, he put his hand on my shoulder, and took me to the side corner of his bedroom and said, "Listen, little tyke..."

120

"Joslin, sir," I interrupted, shaking his hand off of my burnt shoulder.

"... okay, Joslin, this little boy is going to be just fine. I've called a doctor who's just 30 minutes away, lives in a rural spot just off the highway. Up until he gets here, I've been instructed to clean this boy up and take care of him by any means that I can.

"I'm glad that you caught him, to be honest; I couldn't even see him at first with all that dirt caked on, and then I saw you ..."

I didn't mention that I whole-heartedly believed that he was my brother. I was in Owen's custody—my train of thought trekked on to ask myself if I really believed Owen would only hurt **me**. I would never put another soul in danger.

"I think his name is Christian," I said, interrupting him again.

"Well," Eddie said, sighing, "That's good to know, but I need you to listen now."

I **had** been listening. Eddie simply believed Christian's name was irrelevant, so he took the information in as a random five-year-old's comment. I **figured** that the doctor might like to at **least** know his first name...

Eddie continued talking as I thought.

"Joslin, you've got to head off to school. Now, I assure you, you'll be able to visit this boy... Christian... as soon as the school day's over. He's in good hands, and you've been quite the hero today, but you've gotta go now."

I laughed a bit at him, and he glared. "You've got to head to school"... He didn't get it. I never saw school as a mandatory thing. The very idea of him thinking it was

121

mandatory cracked me up.

I didn't have parents. Owen wouldn't know whether I'd gone to school or went playing in the woods. Eddie seemed to care deeply about my "education", nonetheless.

He didn't understand that I was the queen of the whole damn world that day. I'd stood up to the Devil himself. I resented attempts at authority, and Eddie was my second case scenario that day.

Therefore, I didn't give him an answer.

I simply turned.

I felt like I was teaching Owen a lesson again, because I was for damn sure not going to school. It didn't matter to him specifically, but in my rush of adrenaline, adults had their team and I had mine. This day was a game called "defiance" and I was winning.

I started walking toward the marshes opposite from the forests on the other edge of town. That was the place Christian had come from.

*As soon as I came up to the first ghostly tree, I felt a pain in my chest. My heart was literally in pain because the trees—the **trees**, for crying out loud—reminded me of Justin and Eric.*

I rolled my eyes, and reluctantly walked toward the school building.

My small defeat didn't take anything away from my triumph. There would be plenty of time to explore the marsh. It was time to see my family again, and tell them about my new brother.

Most kids would say that I was lucky to have landed in on "free time". My neck and shoulders disagreed with them.

Eric and Justin saw me simultaneously. It was apparent that they were more than ecstatic to see me as their smiles busted out like fireworks. They both gave me a massive hug at the same time.

Oh, yeah, sure, I felt warm and loved, but I also had to bite my lip to avoid screaming at the pressure on the bruise. It felt like they were driving heavy weights into every surface area of my neck, and on top of that, the scratches and burns that were there felt like they were refabricating.

I bit into my lip so hard, it bled, and wouldn't stop. I looked like a retarded fish, slurping my bottom lip into my mouth all day long, but it wasn't uncommon for kindergarteners to do weird things and not care about it.

For example, I've seen kids holding their hands up for forever. Their arms get tired, so they hold one arm up with the other hand. Then, after they've been like that for a while, they start swaying back and forth rapidly like a flopping fish, as if that would help them out in any way.

Anyway, Justin acted ridiculous all day long, hugging and squeezing me, and fluffing my hair. I tried to appear as though it didn't bother me.

"Hey, you don't wanna catch that flu bug I've got!" I said.

"I'm not afraid of germs."

I was so annoyed with him that I decided I would not spend the day with him. I could spend the night at Eric's house, but I just needed to make sure that Justin wasn't invited. Justin's pestering made the school day drag on.

My open window to talk to Eric happened during math time. We had small worksheets with pictures to work on. He was sitting to my right and a little girl named

123

April was sitting to my left.

"Psst. Eric."

"Joslin, it's time to work on math. I don't want to be in Kindergarten forever." Eric was supposed to be in second grade already, after all.

"Okay, I get that... have you noticed Justin though?"

"Yeah, he's flir... yeah, he's acting weird today, huh?"

"Yeah, and I was thinking, you could make an excuse to not hang out with him tonight. I already have my "sick" excuse... I'd like to hang out with you."

April raised her hand abruptly when I finished talking. I held my breath, thinking of what a weasel she was if she were to rat me out for talking. I had plans and no tolerance for some little girl to ruin them.

"Yes?" said the teacher.

"Can I go pee?" said April.

April was an interesting character. I would've asked her to be an ally of mine, but she seemed to want nothing to do with anything or anyone. When she needed to talk, she was polite and sweet, and when she didn't, she still smiled softly.

She never did any work in school unless it was to do with art. In fact, she doodled and sketched on any worksheet, and quite often on the desk, but she'd erase those immediately after completion.

"You may use the restroom." Said the teacher.

As she replied to April's request, she tilted her head to the side. Even as April walked out of sight, the teacher looked at me for a long time, which stopped Eric from responding to me.

"Joslin?"

"Yes, teacher?" I said, getting very nervous and irritable.

"Have you been here all day?" she asked.

"No, just came in at free time." I shrugged.

"Well, I have to count you absent for the day, then, and you'll have to take a note back to your parents."

I glared at her, "Okay."

"And, Joslin, what happened to your neck?" she asked sternly.

Everyone in the room turned to me, and my eyes grew wide. I was wearing the hoodie still, but a little redness was showing above the ties while the hood was down.

That top sliver of scarring could pass off as a rash, so I said, "My flu gave me a rash... I had the flu..."

Then, I noticed everyone's head turn away from me, they had all been staring at me still, wondering what was going on, and literally sticking their noses where they didn't belong.

Even after the opportunity to talk came, and a full conversation could've passed between us, Eric wouldn't talk to me. He bashfully hid behind his own shoulder, like he did before I introduced myself the first time.

*April came back into the room and glared at me a little, and right then, I officially didn't feel good. **She hadn't even been there** when the teacher embarrassed me with her brash statement!*

Unlike everyone else though, she wasn't distant and discrete, but instead, she glared, stuck her tongue out at me, and then started drawing again, but with an angst that I've never seen in her before.

125

April was never like that, so I began to sweat a little. Distraught and uncomfortable, I almost began to worry about the off-balance of the entire universe. Every second on the clock felt like an hour.

Finally, after a strenuous reading period, it was time for the Kindergarteners to get their bags. I grabbed my duffle, and was about to leave with my boys, when the teacher softly grabbed my shoulder.

The small touch felt like pins and needles... with fire at the tips. It seemed they'd formed a shape of a hand and softly pushed into my skin.

Earlier that day, Eddie had touched me with more force when he wanted to talk, but when Teacher touched my skin, it had started to tenderize after a day of hugging and the attempts at healing.

"Here, Joslin, dear, I just need you to take this," said she.

I still wasn't fond of her, personally, and my new hatred for authority made it worse. So, even as I tried to smile, I glared at her, "It's a form to let me know that your parents knew where you were during your absence and why."

As she said that, I caught Justin waving at me and smiling as Eric and him skipped out. I figured they'd just left me.

"I'll have them sign it," I said as I finally cracked a pathetic version of something that was supposed to resemble a smile.

She beamed at me, "Thank you, sweetie."

I nodded, and trudged out of there.

"Hey!" said Eric's voice.

I was surprised to see the two boys smiling at me

when I walked outside the doors.

"Hey, I thought you guys left." I said.

"Well, gosh, not without you, Jos." Justin said.

I grinned, but also rolled my eyes a little.

"So, where do you guys wanna go first?" said Justin.

"Well, actually," Eric chimed in before I could, "I have to get home, my grandpa wanted me to spend some time with him..." he said, rolling his eyes.

"Oh," I said, "Well, actually, I just don't feel very great. I'm gonna go ahead and scat too."

Justin seemed very distressed and disappointed, and even though I was bothered by him earlier today, I still adored him, so I said, "Tomorrow we'll spend like the entire day together!"

"We have school tomorrow..."

"We had school **today**," I retorted, "and I just can't muster up any energy to go anywhere and then go back home."

It surprised me: I could lie so well

Justin still looked dejected, and like he didn't believe me, which was fitting because I lied to him, but I still felt bad about it.

"I guess I'll just get myself home then... see you guys."

There was one more painful hug that I received, and since I couldn't help but wince, I made Justin feel even worse. He was just torn up inside, and I hated it.

I told myself that he'd be fine though. He might be extra sensitive, but he could handle a day more of not seeing me.

The three of us split up at the same time. I wished that Eric would've talked to me during math time, because then we could've set up a place to meet. I absolutely had to visit Christian, and Eric would have to wait. It wasn't fair, because I was the one making plans, but it was the way it had to be.

As Eric pretended to go home, walking off to his grand-pa's house, I made my way towards the bar. Justin was already out of sight, poor fellah, but Eric saw me. He raised a brow, but kept walking, shrugging his shoulders.

I made a dash.

Christian was the only thing on my mind, and as soon as I could, I had to know if he was alright, and then ask him how he could be my brother, and what he knew of our parents.

I had to ask him where he'd been all that time. Perhaps our parents thought he was dead and gave up a search for him when I was born.

I had to consider all scenarios.

Through the swinging wild-west-styled bar doors I went, and without consulting anyone, I ran around and behind the counter, up the stairs, and through the hallway.

On Eddies bed was the same jungle boy I saw before. Barely recognizable with his eyes so clear, and his body and hair washed thoroughly. Christian sat upright and stared at me. So, I sat down and stared right back.

Keeping my gaze, and losing concentration, I finally spoke, "How are you feeling, Christian?"

He answered immediately, "I feel great! No problems here. And how are **you** doin'?"

I waited for him to say my name after the pause, but it wasn't a pause.

"Christian doesn't really know me…" I thought to myself.

"Err… I'm doing just fine." I said, "Christian?"

"Yessum?"

"What's your last name?"

Christian didn't hesitate to say the ridiculous phrase, "I don't know."

And at the point of awareness of life I'd reached (as a five-year-old), I was unmoved by his apparent amnesia. I thought nothing of its rarity, solely disturbed by its inconvenient irony.

He could've been my brother, but neither of us knew who he was.

In fact, my first thought was, "It figures," which, I verbalized.

"What?" Christian asked.

"Well, Christian, I think I'm your little sister, but I don't know if I am or not. See, my name is Joslin, and I…"

"Wait!" he shouted, and startled, I jumped back.

Noting the pulse, he said, "Sorry," then back on track, he said, "I know that name!"

I grinned. "You do?"

My heart started racing a little, and Christian got up from the bed where he was sitting.

Like Eric, Christian's hugs felt as warm as my father's, but the difference was that when Christian was standing, he was as tall as Father used to be (when he'd take a knee) to hug.

"Thank you for saving me." Christian whispered.

In his embrace, although I was disheartened to

not have all the answers I wanted, I was so happy. Blood or not, Christian was my brother. I felt happy and safe with him, unlike any feeling I'd had before.

He was family, and I would stand up for him, no matter what.

"You're welcome, bro." I said, grinning again.

"Bro?" he asked.

"Yeah." I said, smiling as I started toward the door (hearing Eddie's footsteps down the hall), "Why not? Seems to me you'd be a good brother."

Christian laughed, "Alright then, see ya tomorrow, sis!"

"See ya!"

Upon saying those two words, I ran face first into Eddie's knee.

Eddie looked down at me sternly, "Joslin."

"Eddie?" I replied.

He didn't say anything else, just stood in my way.

"Okay, look." I said.

Eddie cracked a smile. No doubt it was funny seeing a puny five-year-old acting so tough and so serious. I got the reactions a lot, but it was a new experience for Eddie.

"I was just up here to check up, I know I'm trespassing. I will go now."

Eddie tipped his Yankee's baseball cap, "See you around, ma'am" he said, beaming.

I smiled back at him, and then gave Christian one last wave goodbye and trotted down the stairs. When I exited through the swinging doors, Eric was leaning *against the entryway like a cowboy without a hat.*

"Hey!" I shouted.

Eric looked up, "Hey! What took you so long, drunkard?"

I laughed, "Boy, do I have things to tell you! Let's go to your place."

I told him about Christian, and he listened. He didn't seem quite as excited about the Tip Sod Tarzan I'd found.

So, since the subject didn't linger, I asked him about other things during the walk there.

What he thought about April's reaction:

He asked me who April was.

"She's an almost-ally, I think." My eyes narrowed, "You're kind of thick, aren't you?" and I smiled.

"Hey! What? Why?" He yelled, surprised by my blunt insult.

"Well, it's obvious that she's a cool person, I don't get why you haven't acquainted yourself with her."

"Um. Jos, that doesn't make me stupid. I just don't care about people until they start caring about me."

There was a long pause in our conversation as I contemplated Eric's personality.

"Why do you call your friends allies?" he said after a while.

"Well, friends are for company. Allies are more part of a team. We help each other out, you, me, and Justin. I can't just call you guys 'friends'."

He smiled, "Good answer."

Back through the magical, train-tunnel-like, plant-infested doorway we went, to Sheriff Shutter's house. As we came to the gate once again, I thought about how just that morning I'd seen Cain Shutter tripping over himself drunk. It made me a little nervous for a moment, but I shook it off.

Obviously, not everyone acted the same when drunk, and a drunk, tipsy, or hung-over Cain Shutter was better than a sober Owen Tilda any day.

Eric and I climbed the fence, and went inside.

His grandpa was passed out on the sofa in the living room, with WWE blasting on the television. The announcers were talking about how "juuuuust two years ago was the BICENTENNIAL SHOWDOWN!" And the television displayed, "flashback action shots" of "legendary monsters!" (They were really just men with horrifically giant muscles).

Another word Eric knew, that I didn't was "bicentennial". I figured it out as he muttered, "Two hundred years, holy shoot!"

He was pulling me gently by my hand, taking me to his room, which I'd glanced at, but never really saw it.

As he and I sat down (crisscross applesauce), I prepared myself for what I was about to unload.

Eric was pleasant, and as I started explaining everything that happened since my arrival to Tip-Sod town, his smile faded, but to my relief he didn't look too alarmed.

He interrupted me once, just to say he knew I was too graceful to be so klutzy. It was a completely unneeded, but appreciated ego-boost that made me laugh.

I felt like I could trust him, and I was right. He was

very calm and even chuckled. He spoke normally, as if I weren't in imminent danger.

"You actually believe in that stuff?" he said, when I told him Owen was the Devil. He chuckled a little more.

"It's true! What else is he then?"

"A very messed up guy." Eric replied.

"I don't think anything human could hurt another in such a way."

"Joslin, if you can't believe in Heaven, then don't believe in Hell! (I've heard that it's not such a fun place.)" He nudged my shoulder, "And Satan? I mean, do you seriously think a little red man with horns on his head is inside yer uncle?"

This description of the Devil was one I had never heard of before. It was like one of the children in our kindergarten class had drawn a cartoon in my mind when he described it to me, and I had to laugh at him.

"Where did you hear that?"

"Hear what?"

He was confused. I explained to him that the Devil was not simply a person, and he was definitely not colored red and given horns. In the books I'd been read Lucifer had originally been an angel, but he wanted to go up against God.

Eric laughed and said, "The old man with the white beard in the sky?"

Eric was hysterical.

I didn't mention to him that in my mind God, was just all of the good things of the world and the Devil was all the bad. I didn't want to admit that I didn't fully understand the phenomenon that God and the Holy Ghost and Jesus were.

I'd never gone to church; I just read a few stories and passages in some books. I was laughing too hard to concentrate on anything, anyway, thinking of Eric's version of the Devil.

The point is that my visit to Eric had lifted my spirits completely, and I couldn't ask for a better ally, or friend.

We talked more in depth about the things that we'd been through. Eric's father would throw him across the hall and smack him around. He didn't end up with many bruises, but the pain was awful, and Eric had been my age back then. His grandfather saved him over a year before, when he was six.

I thought Eric's story made mine seem so brutal.

It wasn't until I was finished telling him about my life with my parents that we argued about who had the better end of the deal. Eric said he had never been loved by anyone in his life and I said that my abuse was far more painful than his.

His defense was, "You don't know that!" and he got very offended too.

It was almost as if he wanted to beat me at having things worse off. But then, I disproved his side of the argument.

He settled down when I said, "You're wrong because I love you."

The mood lightened, and Eric put down his pathetic defenses in order to grin wickedly. He laughed, "Don't say that to me in front of Justin."

"What?" I asked, "I love you? Why?"

He smiled wide, ear-to-ear, "Never-you-mind." Then he became serious again, "Did you tell Justin about Owen?"

"No... should I?"

He shook his head vigorously, "No way, Justin understood my story, but I think that since you're actually getting beat up right now, he's gonna tell his dad."

I was suspicious.

Eric and Justin were feuding over me, and that night, supplied by my skepticism on whether or not I should tell Justin, I finally gained an awareness of their "crushes".

I slept there in Eric's room that night, and left the room before he awoke in the morning.

I managed to make it into my room and back to school the next day in one piece. For once Owen didn't even notice I was gone. For the first time a drunken fluke on his part brought some good luck to me...

After school the next day, Justin, Eric and I slept over in the Diner. The night went fast, because the fun lasted throughout. There was nothing to think about.

We went outside to play a game that we invented called, "King of the Forest". It consisted of one of us wearing a toque with twigs poking out from the fold. That person was the king. They were supposed to find their "subjects" (the other two players) and the beasts of the forest (some bunny rabbits or whatever else lurked around). It was a game of hide-and-seek where you never changed who was the seeker because "you could never find all of the beasts of the forest".

It was Justin's turn to be the king, and he found "his subjects" right away. Afterwards, the subjects must help the king find all of the beasts.

Every time we ever played the game, the king was supposed to create a storyline to go with the game. Justin's involved a treacherous tree's kidnapping spree,

135

and his minions o' plenty.

We ran and laughed until our sides and guts hurt. We frequently made funny faces at animals. At one point the game even took a turn and we all jumped up on different trees and shouted things.

Such as, "Hah! I have vanquished this one! Feel the sting of my royal sword!" Justin said, poking his enemy in the bark with a stick that he plucked from its very branch.

Eric busted out in laughter, "That sounds so wrong!"

Justin and I were oblivious to Eric's play on his words, "Well, it isn't. The tree deserved it!"

Eric just grinned and snapped back into play-mode. He spied a tree that had fallen, mounted it and yelled, "One, TWO, THREE, we've got a winner," he lifted his own hand in the air, as he stood on top of his opponent. Then he jumped down and cupped his hands over his mouth, mocking the sound of a vast crowd watching a wrestling match.

I stood atop my tree and shouted, "Now see, your men depend on your surrender, otherwise, they shall all be slain."

I felt a little weird talking to the trees like that. I mean, I was an odd little girl, and I talked to them anyways, but I had never been their enemy, but in the moment, it humored me.

Having fun with Justin again and looking at that spark in his eye made me feel guilty.

*"My past with Owen shouldn't bring on guilt at all," I thought, "and it technically isn't **anyone's** business." My thoughts legitimized my secrecy, but the guilt didn't fade. In a matter of speaking, I simply had put*

it on "the back burner".

There, I let the thought fester for weeks. In the meantime, there were other things to concentrate on.

Winter calmed the earth in Alabama. It wasn't cold enough to bring snow, but the chill was enough, to give one a good week-long cold. This happened to everyone in class except for me.

I'd never gotten a virus or germ in my life. I've felt sick before, but that's not the same thing. The human brain can bring about sickness without help from an outside source, just from chemicals and emotion. I've never been truly sick though. The year 2143 didn't change that.

My sixth birthday passed in January, and I ended up completely ignoring it. Then as time passed and lapsed simultaneously (as it only seems to do when you're bored) spring crept up on us. Owen had left me to myself for the winter months...

During the months that ended Kindergarten, I tried again and again to visit Eric at night. I walked close to his window to peek in and see if he was awake, but he never was. So, instead, I went to my secret place in the forest.

Street lamps lit the way for me and it was partially comforting, except that whenever the wind moved, I was nearly positive that it was Owen creeping about in the shadows. Yet, streetlights and long eerie shadows didn't exist in the little jungle on the edge of Tip Sod town.

There, in that beautiful kingdom of secretive creatures and natural tree-houses, I had a sense of power and structure. I felt like I could never break down and never grow tired or old. I felt free.

I **became** free. In the tree-house that someone had built before my time, I'd sleep on many occasions. Sometimes for weeks on end I'd camp there, and Owen couldn't touch me.

The only word that I can think of to describe that is "blissful".

I had to of course come to the house for some food, and to appear there once in a while just so Owen never came looking for me, but otherwise, I felt safe the whole year. Owen didn't hurt me again until first grade. He seemed to be distant from me, always thinking about something else. And that was **fine** by me!

Days went by and kindergarten went fast, except when I felt the guilt again. I felt that way, because I met Justin first, and he offered help that I didn't except out of biased thoughts. He had the potential to be trusted, and because of Eric's opinion, I never gave him the chance.

Also, Eric didn't help my guilt… it was almost as if he considered us to be better friends because of our secret. Eric didn't realize how I felt; I just hated keeping things from Justin. There was a sort of earnest in his eyes that I never wanted to fail.

Thankfully, during the summer, I developed a distraction.

I was sitting alone one day in my tree house, looking up at the cloud patterns in the sky. I was thinking about how life interested me, when suddenly I heard twigs snapping and the ground shuffling below.

I was compelled to start playing a game of "fort" with this new stranger, considering that the circumstances were perfect.

"A trespasser?" I whispered.

"Who goes there!?" I shouted.

Miranda, looked up, and met my lethal stare with her eyes and said, "The trees are different here."

Her eyes looked foggy and dilated, and she appeared to be opening them as wide as she could. "I mean, I've seen plenty of similar trees in Yorubaland, but these seem to be surrounded with entangling plants and they grow in slightly different formations..."

"Hey!" I shouted, interrupting her rant.

She looked back up at me, glaring, "What do you want, sickie?"

"I beg yer pardon?" I said. As Justin might've said: 'them are fightin' words'. I guessed it was fitting to use an uncouth southern accent when someone insulted you in such a way.

"Well, you're just one of those examples I've seen of Mother Earth's abominable sickness." Said the little black girl, "So many pale human beings are in this land, and they've infected Nigeria as well."

Well, it was my turn to glare. As a little genius, thanks to the books my father read to me, and my fast learning capabilities, I knew a bit about demographics through the ages. The truth in history from 20 to twenty-hundred years ago was something my parents indulged in and studied frequently along with the common fantasies.

As far as Europe goes, it's been mostly "white" throughout the ages. The United States was a melting pot, but the biggest three groups were Mexican-Americans, European-Americans (your basic "mutts") African-Americans and Asians on the coasts. Asia has always had mostly just tourists and Asians.

Africa *though, Africa had a subtly growing "white" population for centuries.*

The remnants from the struggle over settlements

139

in the 1800's have created a European-African melting pot, and this was no news in the year 2142. However, the amount of white people had dwindled over the last half-century to nearly naught (don't ask me why), so I couldn't expect Miranda to recognize diversity when she saw it.

Still, she should've seen enough white people to know that we were... around.

"I'm not sick." I said.

"Yeah, yeah, that's what my mom told me about you people too, but she's a little sickly as well." She said, her eyes out of focus, staring into the woods.

I hopped from a branch in my tree near the ladder, landed on my feet and stuck my hand out.

"Pleased to meet you, lady, my name is Joslin."

Miranda grabbed my hand right away, making me feel like I was sheltered. How was it that I was the only girl unfamiliar with the popularity of hand shaking?

"Well, I'mma go now. My mom and I just moved in with this guy in the city. She's enrolling me in the school over here now, but she should be done in a bit."

"Hold on!" I said, "Aren't you going to tell me your name?"

"No," she said.

The inner turmoil she appeared to have over the subject of a name didn't really seem necessary, so I excused her from my thoughts when she turned to leave.

She spoke very clear English compared to some of the other black children I'd encountered. It seemed that in this part of Alabama, white people had a terribly confusing accent most of the time, but a lot of the black children took it to the next level, creating an impalpable language.

She had a thick accent, and she her consonants pressed hard on the air when she spoke, but it was a lot easier to understand than creole.

It was odd for her to be joining in on our school year when we only had ten days left. I was determined to not miss a day of school, so that I could recognize her purpose in all of my recent circumstances.

I ended up figuring absolutely nothing about her out during those ten days, because she wasn't even in our grade. She was in third grade, but she really didn't look that old.

So, yes, I shortly forgot about the girl I'm now living with. A lot can change in eleven years.

Besides, it was easy to forget about a stranger when a friend was trying to permanently distance himself from me. On the last day of school, Justin got into a fight with Eric, and wouldn't talk to me (which wasn't very fair to me).

I asked Eric what he and Justin were arguing about when they were at the drinking fountain. All Eric did was tell me not to worry about it, and then he also stopped talking to me.

We all left the school building by ourselves for the first time since I'd arrived in Tip Sod Town.

So, unconventionally, I visited Christian for the second time ever after school.

I decided that I needed some brotherly advice, but this time, I marched up to the Bar, expecting a big welcome from Christian.

I pushed past the swinging bar doors, and walked up to the counter. I eyeballed a bar stool for a while when I stood there waiting. I decided my upper arm strength wasn't to a level where I'd be able to prop myself up with ease... I couldn't help but try it out anyway—I was a very stubborn child.

As I slipped and fumbled with the bar stool, I saw Christian pop his head up from behind the counter, "So, what'll it be, sis?"

I was so fixated on trying to conquer the bar stool that his voice startled me, and I fell to the floor. Christian laughed at me. He laughed as if my physical blunder was the most hilarious thing in the world.

I figured that about a minute into the laughter, he'd be done, but he wasn't.

I had to interrupt him, "Christian! Are you drunk?"

"Uh... yeah. Proballery."

"You are probably like what? 10?"

"I'm nine, I think actually, but I can go for being ten, in the life... I am. I mean, snot like I can eh-member."

"Okay, well, that's not the point. I'm six years old. I shouldn't have to be telling you that alcohol is bad for you, first off, and also, it's illegal for you to be drinking it."

"Well, woopi-doo-loo! Look who's talking! I just served the Sheriff a beer and hour 'go, whaddaya thinka that, little missy?"

His mouth was cracked open to the left and his eyebrows were raised really high in this weird-ass grin that I didn't like. His hair was silky-smooth, but very unkempt purposely, and wrapped in a loose ponytail.

Don't get me wrong, it was a hilarious moment, but I wasn't there to talk to an idiot.

I raised a brow, stepped down from the platform that held the bar and gave Christian his space for the time being. I didn't know if Eddie knew what Christian was doing, or if maybe he put him up to it, but I'd deal with the situation later.

I was very disappointed in the boys in my life. They were the only people in my life, really, and I felt them all pushing me away.

So, I ran "home" to the black oak house that my captor owned. I've been hurt by Owen many times, but he never punched me.

Abruptly, as I slipped through the door, my face was punted into play by Owen's fist. The occurrence played through my head right away and rather unexpectedly, I completely busted out in laughter.

I could feel my face heal immediately; I didn't even know which part was hit.

Owen just looked at me with astonishment, and I immediately stopped everything, even breathing, and stared right back at him.

For at least a minute, we stayed locked in the same positions, looking at each other, both of us equally afraid.

Then, suddenly, I felt myself grinning again, and I hopped up to my feet and dashed up the creaking steps, made it to my room and slammed the door.

My heart was pounding, harder and harder as I attempted to catch my breath. My throat began to dry up, so I shut my mouth and held my breath momentarily, and within that moment, I heard a rattling noise from above me.

I gasped. And as I breathed, the rattling stopped.

With my breathing slowed and moderated, I tried holding my breath again to hear that same noise and it worked. The rattling was coming from the ceiling, but not directly above me.

My brain was stirring with endorphins from that weird moment of laughter, and now this confounded curiosity, and I felt like I'd been put under a spell.

The curiosity over-took my entire being.

I took a deep breath and walked into the hallway where the rattling became clearer and clearer to me.

I breathed for about five seconds, fast, and then held back. The noise continued until I had to gasp at the other noises behind me. Owen's footsteps in his heavy black boots were following me. The sound eluded me until it was too late.

A tight grip of ice-cold fingers on my neck lifted me up so high that the top of my head touched the ceiling. My tiny feet wiggled beneath me and my airway was completely constricted.

"Do you hear it?" he said, "Do you hear yourself?"

Of course, while I was turning blue, I couldn't answer the question that was rhetorical anyway and made no sense to me.

"Why can I HEAR IT... but gain NOTHING from it?" he screamed, bringing me down so that we came nose to nose.

Then he dropped me, and I gasped. I coughed from breathing in too fast with my crushed pharynx. There was so much pressure in my head that I felt like I could see my neck glowing.

Owen was there... it couldn't possibly be glowing... I was healing in front of Owen?

Owen stood still, his face emotionless. The typical crazed look vanished and he softly whispered something as he looked at each one of the doors in the hallway.

I tried to cry. My gut felt in need of it. And

although tears naturally came to my eyes, I didn't get the satisfaction I desired. My innards were in knots, and I couldn't move for the longest time.

Owen scoffed, at what I don't know, but I also didn't care.

I was aware that he was keeping a secret from me, but as far as I knew he'd been keeping it for forever, and who was I to even care about his issues.

Still... it was about that curious noise...

That noise that seemed to be connected to my life, to my own breathing pattern—Owen thought it was important. Capable of doing something for me.

Still, I couldn't get to whatever was making the noise as long as he was there to stop me. So I ceased my pursuit, and I continued laying there as Owen turned abruptly and walked calmly down the steps.

The pain I felt was overwhelming.

I didn't want to breathe. I wanted to die. I wished to close my eyes and die and be with my mother. I wanted to hold my real father, and stop these reminders of them.

The people that I couldn't depend on, whose hugs engulfed me in my own stupor were involved with my memories of something that could never be duplicated or redone. And my allies had turned against me when it turned out I needed them most.

My mind started to go places I feared to think of directly, and I couldn't stop it. I wanted to die and never have a memory again. I wanted to leave this world of disappointments and pain. I wanted to kill myself.

Suddenly as I thought that, I drifted into a dream-state. I journeyed into a reoccurring dream that I thought I'd lost with the death of my parents.

"The small white creatures touched my skin. They danced a ballet into my pores and swarmed about infecting my blood...

The creatures were a part of me; they weren't magic nor were they the maggots they portrayed, but something to construct me.

I never dreamed of them... I was made of them..."

The dream seemed to last less than a second, but I knew better than that. Something changed... something happened to me while I was dreaming...

The pain had entirely vanished from my neck. I stood up and walked over to the bathroom. When I peeled off the hoodie and examined my neck, the process of the healing stunned me. There was no bruise from our most recent incident here in the hallway, and even the old burns had changed into a curative, scarring wound.

Scabbing and discoloration littered my skin like disgusting piles of rubble on an old lot. Yellow faded into bluish black and purple scabs stuck out from the old infected lines of blood.

I couldn't stand it anymore. I slunk back into my hoodie, being careful not to touch the fabric to my skin. The pain had finally subsided, but the scabs snagged and broke a little when they touched the inner fabric.

I wanted to itch at them so badly, but I resisted.

Then, in a tornado of panicky thoughts, I decided to sneak out and find Eric.

I had to talk to someone; otherwise, I might've just exploded with the frustration I withheld but Owen was downstairs—possibly guarding the doorway.

That didn't seem very likely. Truthfully, he was most likely sitting in his easy chair, filling up on beer, but I wasn't prepared to take any more risks. On the off chance he was blocking me from my freedom, I avoided going down the stairs.

I even made sure that my breath didn't waver at any moment, so that I didn't conjure up the mysterious noise again. I stepped out of my own window, and onto the roof. Luckily for me, there was a tree, whose branches grew so expansively that one of them was almost poking in through a window to that room in the house I'd left unexplored.

So as I continued to fight an overlord of curiosity, I climbed into the tree, and slid down to the ground on the truck. I didn't quite know how to navigate my way through the forest that cut off the highway and dispersed into the town, so to save time, I risked being caught on the road in front of the house.

My heart was pounding so loud in my chest, I felt like he'd hear it. The lights in Owens house were all on, and I felt like the door might open at any moment. In the moment, it was as if I was escaping a beast about to swallow me whole. That house could open its trap, and never let me out!

Thankfully, I made it across the highway and onto the dirt road.

The springtime air was sticky and sweet with

magnolia scents. Ironically, the smells were usually gross outside; up until today the air had smelled like mold and sweat. Perhaps it was just my mind concentrating on positives to distract myself. I couldn't be sure.

I ran as fast as I could, and made it to the Sheriff's office. It was locked of course and come to think of it there wasn't an excuse for me to even try the front except for how flustered I was: I couldn't think clearly.

The back entryway was wide open. Through the tunnel I could see that the gate was oddly unlocked. I crept forward, and for some reason I felt more like I was trespassing now than I did before when we climbed the fence. I guess the key word was "we" and being with my allies always made me feel safe.

Through the open gate, I walked solely and cautiously. When gazing at the door, I spotted a little note, covering the hole in the brick wall.

"Eric and I are off to Florida. Be there for about until his schooling starts, visiting his cousins and Aunt Mariel. Left the key in that space and be sure to watch out for Buster, Ken. Thank you for looking after the office while I'm gone. —S. Cain Shutter"

"Damn." I thought.

I walked out into the clearing outside the fence, and sat for a minute. I was wearing my hoodie still, even though the night was hot and sticky, and sweat was creeping at my neck and torso. I pondered my next move. Going back to Owen's—not an option.

Justin's name hovered in my head, and I had a small war with myself while deciding whether or not to run into him...

Intelligence and knowledge don't rid one of

148

confusion. Only experience can do that. Then the experience will go on to morph itself into wisdom. I had very little wisdom at my age, because I had very little experience.

...I had no idea how to talk to someone like Justin, or if the idea was wise in the first place. He was so sensitive.

Against my doubts and better judgment I stood up and started walking toward the Diner. Then, much to my surprise, a large force knocked me off my feet and to the ground. I had a sharp pain on my forehead and my back arched in a wrong way, so I couldn't get up.

Then after a moment I healed from the fracture completely. I felt "healthy as a horse" as -whoever- would say. I jumped up straight away, to see what force of nature attacked me.

Justin shook the dust from his red head and squinted at me through the darkness. He was illuminated by a patch of light from the streetlamp.

"Joslin?" he said.

I stepped into the light with him.

"Did I hurt you?" he asked, pulling my black hair behind my ear.

"Well, at first my head hurt," I said truthfully, then snorted, "but I don't appear to be bleeding."

"Hmm... let's check to be sure," he smiled, pulling my face in close to his by gripping the back of my head. His fingernail scratched my neck scratches a little and I winced, biting my lip again.

"Well, there appears to be no damage. Hah, sorry if I scratched you there. Anyways, long time no see, huh? We never hung out, you an' me."

149

"Sure we did! That night we played "King of the Forest" in the Diner, we were all having a **great** time!"

"Yeah, but that was with..." He paused, "**you** wanna hang out now?"

"Sure! That's actually where I was heading."

I thought long and hard about what I was about to do and say. First off, I laughed at myself in my head a little for my former petty complaints about Justin. The humor was replaced with anxiety quickly, because I was determined to tell Justin my secret tonight.

"I was wondering why you were out here." Justin said, giggling.

"Well, now it's your turn! What were you doing out here? And why were you running?"

"Oh, well, my dad's house-sitting for Eric's grandpa, and... I uh... I got scared of being alone, I guess."

I had the most ridiculous flash back when he said that. I flashed-back to a time just before I turned five, when my father was always away, and my mother sometimes left me alone during the day. It was never for over an hour (I was that woman's world).

But anyway, I knew exactly what Justin was talking about. I, too, was afraid of being alone, and I empathized with him.

Not that I'd say this way back then, but to put it straight to the point, my time with Owen turned me into a hard-ass. I'm positive that had I not been through all that hard core horror with him, I would've had the hugest crush on Justin. We had a lot of similarities. I probably would have talked to him more and certainly never would've found my own ally to be annoying.

I smiled, "Well, I'll be here with you."

Justin smiled back, showing off bloody gums where a front tooth used to be. He must've hit my head harder than I thought.

"Hey, I really got you good, didn't I?" I laughed, "you get a visit from the tooth faerie!"

"The what, now?"

"Oh, Lordy, don't tell me you've never heard of her!"

This mythical creature had a background story which was one of my favorites from my father, because unlike the others, he told it without having to read it. Thusly, I decided, there was a better chance that he was telling the truth. He looked into my eyes when he told it, and the details were impeccably realistic.

As we walked I gave Justin a brief summary of the story, and he listened without saying a word.

All of the dirt and gravel stones clicked beneath our shoes. My hoodie, saturated in my sweat, clung onto my skin. The smell underneath was nothing short of revolting.

As Justin said, "Whoa." Or wow, or something in reaction to the story, I was nervous that he'd started to smell me.

Immediately, I retorted, "Hey, you guys have a bath in your bathroom, right?"

I remember having to ask this, and I'm actually kind of shocked that I never "had to go" there before and didn't know this information already.

"Well, duh."

"Well, gee!" I laughed, pushing his shoulder, "I was just wondering,"

We made it to the front doors, "... could I borrow

some of your clothes, and take a shower here? You'd have your clothes back before the summer is over for sure. I could maybe bring them by tomorrow if I'm allowed out."

"Well," He said, opening the door, a subtle line of worry or nervousness starting on his forehead as we walked inside, "Uh… er… do you have a bathtub at your house?"

"Well, yeah," I said, "I just don't really feel like going back there, and coming back here… it's just a bit of a hassle."

"I'm pretty sure everybody has a bathtub at their house." Justin lost some of his edginess in that sentence, stable enough to stop stuttering and poke fun at me.

I laughed, "Well, come on though, Justin, it's not like you live in a normal house. It wasn't **that** stupid of a question. Unless all eating places include bathtubs in the restroom."

"What's that word Eric uses? Touché? You're right. But still. It's not like we wouldn't have a bathtub."

When we came to the dark hallway, Justin started to get nervous again, and looked down at his shoes.

After a while of looking at his speckled face, waiting for him to speak, I opened my mouth to say something, and he interrupted with one of his nervous outbursts, "So I'll go get you a towel and set out some clothes!"

I saw his green eyes blink, I blinked, and he ran off. I didn't understand his anxiety and I didn't know where it came from.

But, he was back in a flash, with towel in hand, and a hairdryer, and clothing underneath his armpit.

"Well, thank you!" I said, grabbing everything awkwardly. The sweatpants came unfolded, and the *hairdryer cord slipped loose.*

"Yeah, those are some of my mom's pj's she left behind, 'cept the sweatpants belong to me. I, uh, wasn't too sure what you wanted or how comfortable you'd be in..."

"Justin, I'm uncomfortable now. I'll take whatever you've got. Are you sure it's okay for me to wear your mom's stuff?"

"Well, dad's not going to care, if that's what you mean..."

So, I shrugged, nodded and took a bath.

I scrubbed like hell on my neck, making it sting and bleed. The steam from the scalding water loosened the dead patches of skin, but I itched so badly. The anger from having to put up with everything was lashed out with the gripping and scratching at my decaying skin, tearing my outer layer apart.

When I drained the water, I turned the showerhead on and watched the suds and residue from my neck's extraneous scabbing traveling down the drain along with some fresh glowing blood.

I sneered, wiped myself clean of entrails and scrubbed myself off with the towel. My skin continued to peel off and I felt like I hadn't even gotten clean.

*After getting into the shower repeatedly and back out again, I finally decided that I had to just **be clean enough**. I started tiring out and I hadn't even talked to Justin yet.*

I shook the towel out rapidly, and brushed off any pieces I found left behind, and then shook it out again for extra measure.

"Ugh!" I shouted at no one.

153

I wrapped my hair up in the towel, and put on the sweatpants. The shirt Justin picked out had a funny looking picture of a dog on it, so I laughed.

I looked at myself in the mirror as I slipped the shirt on.

My neck was just raw skin and blood spots that appeared more painful than they were.

So I started to cry.

And I cried loudly.

I was so sick of that hoodie, the towel was so dirty, and I was sick of being hurt. Truthfully, I felt I didn't need any other reason to cry after having held myself together so well for so long.

It wasn't long before Justin knocked on the door.

So, I opened it, and blurted out just one of my many thoughts, "Where is your washing machine?"

Justin looked very frightened. His eyes were wide as he looked at my tarnished neck and yelled, "Joslin!"

I threw my arms around him and cried. "Justin, I'm so fed up! I can't deal with this, and I don't want to keep secrets anymore. I'm just afraid. I don't want you to tell anyone, I don't want them to send me away! Who knows what's going to happen to me? Besides, Owen won't be killed like he deserves. I want him to... I want him to die!"

I never even knew that thought had crossed my mind, but it had and it was true. The violence in my heart was passionate and pure. I wanted Owen to die. My life would be marvelous if only he would.

Justin, finally moving, grabbed my shoulders and pulled me away, "He did this to you?"

"Yes..." I said looking at the blood I left on his

154

neck. It glowed white, then disappeared.

It was my turn to be anxious.

Despite all of my expectations for Justin, he didn't freak out, he didn't tell me, "quick, we've got to go tell my dad..." Justin put his hands on his hips and shook his head.

Then he looked up at me rather coldly, "What can I do, Joslin?"

"What do you mean? I don't want you to do anything..."

"So then what was the point of even telling me about it?" He snapped at me.

I started wailing again.

"Joslin. Stop! Just stop this. Listen to me." He grabbed my hand roughly and pulled me into his bedroom. I was sniffling and gasping uncontrollably.

I couldn't believe it!

I hadn't met up with Justin for his sympathy really, but I expected it, and that had destroyed my shield of invulnerability, and he was harsh with me.

"Listen to me, Jos. I can't help you, alright?"

I couldn't look up at him.

"Hey, look at me, look at these pathetic little arms..." he said.

I looked up and giggled as he flexed his six-year-old arms, and he smiled.

Then he spoke firmly again, "I can't help you by any means. I've already been through one of these issues before. I've already known about one person whose problems I couldn't solve. 'A course, I was there after he'd already solved the issue, but I still felt like I was under pressure and maybe a little unsafe for knowing the information I knew.

"Now, I'm not afraid, but I shouldn't know this if you don't want me to go to a grown-up and try and save you."

"But, Justin!"

He put his finger to my lips, "I'm not done. I shouldn't know; this is what I'm telling you, but you've put your trust in me anyways not to tell.

"Honestly, to tell you the truth, Jos, nobody in this town even cares anyways. They don't care about you, me, or Eric. Everyone here likes to keep to themselves, and I'm warning you that you'll be disappointed in me if you actually do wan' me to help you.

"Because Eric wasn't lying... His grandpa's the sheriff, and he really couldn't give one ounce of care to other people's problems. He just wants to hear the good, the interesting, and the funny. My dad don't care neither, and the same thing goes for any other grown-up here you'll come across."

My sniffles were stifled, and my tears had dried.

Justin hit me with a reality bullet that (like any bullet) was hard to take:

Those who could help me wouldn't and those who would help me couldn't.

Part of me wanted him to be a "rat" and tell, and maybe I'd see everything turn out alright and we'd all make it through- happy. Justin ratting Owen out in all honesty would only bring gossip and a huge beating for me, followed by excruciating captivity. Not to mention, it would put Justin at a huge risk.

After a pause of silence, my unspoken tension, and a sad look on his face, Justin sighed, "So, that's what happened when you were gone for that week?"

I nodded, and he looked closely at the blood and bruising on my neck.

"Did he burn you, Jos?"

"Yeah, but I was unconscious for that part."

Justin's eyes grew wide, and I became uncomfortable.

"Don't treat me any different because of this."

"Why would I do that?" he whined.

"Because you've already started to!"

"Joslin! Ugh! You can't think that I'm just gonna have no reaction. It's not like I'm brushing this thing off. You're being hurt, and there's nothing I can do about it, and then you told me, that's frustrating, and there's nothing you or me can do about that either.

"I'm scared and I'm mad and my gut hurts. I don't want you ever going back home." Justin drew out most of his rant without taking a breath (like your average six-year-old talking about something, afraid they'll forget a word or two).

"And what's going to happen when Owen finds me?"

"I didn't tell you not to go back. I'm not dumb. I actually think you should go now, because he'll pound you into the ground if you don't and he just finds you gone."

"Justin. Please, let me sleep here. Justin, I ran out here to escape. I don't wanna go back." I pleaded.

Something flickered in Justin's eyes and his body pulsed, like I'd just broken a barrier of toughness. His limbs went loose and his eyes flooded.

"Come here, Joslin. I won't let anything happen to you tonight."

I snuggled into him, feeling him sob, and his tears soaked a small section of my hair. When he let his guard down, I would've put up a frontage again, but I didn't need to. I lifted my head and kissed his cheek. I felt him smile.

By that time, I knew that both Eric and Justin liked me... they were "puppy loving" or whatever you want to call it. Their tension was jealousy, which was useless, because I didn't have a crush on either of them.

I smiled with Justin. In my mind I said, "You know, I might as well smile, because this is perhaps the most blissful moment I'll ever have."

We both were dreary-eyed and were talking about sweet nothings and strange nothings alike, "Hey Joslin?"

"Yeah, Justin?"

"I'm sorry... I got mad at you..."

My curiosity peaked. I had been wondering why he stopped talking to me.

"It's okay..." I said.

"Well, Eric told me that you told him a secret... I don't feel anything personal about it. I know why you told him first..."

"Hey, Justin"

"Yeah, Jos?"

"I'm glad I told you afterwards... Really. You're making me feel... okay—better than I have been."

I felt him smile again, and then I said, "Uh, Justin..."

"Hmm?"

"Do you ever feel such a peaceful feeling that you

forget your heart is there inside you?"

"I'm not sure... sounds inter'sting though," he said, gripping my shoulder tighter.

"Well... I'm just so peaceful now, and I just remembered that my heart exists because I felt it squirm inside me, kinda like it was trying to push out toward my very skin... just escape my ribs a little to remind me that I'm a human..."

*Justin didn't have a comment for the longest time, and then he groaned and looked at me, his eyeballs almost touching mine goofily, "You **do** realize that you're only six, right?"*

We both laughed.

▪▪▪

Miranda reenters the house, and finds Joslin asleep on the counter where she'd left her that morning.

Her eyebrows turn to show worry to no one in particular.

Joslin's presence acts as Miranda's vindication for her beliefs at the current moment. She believes that running into her was a miracle of a sign that she'd find her father someday (who ran off long ago).

More than that, Miranda just cares about Joslin in general, and to see the pale, but deeply breathing figure resting on the hard counter is difficult for an old friend.

As Miranda worries, Joslin blithely dreams.

After 'while, I must've fallen asleep there in that little boy's arms. When I woke up, it was to Ken Mlisbled's voice.

He announced, "Justin, I'm making bacon and eggs!"

159

I felt Justin jolt up as if his feet were on fire, "Oh my gosh, Joslin! You're still here!"

I stretched, "I guess I fell asleep. I was really tired."

Justin smiled at that, and then he broke from 'happy go lucky' to, "Jos, you gotta get out, my dad will steam from his head if he sees you in my room."

I snickered, "That'd actually be funny," in my first-grade humor, "like a steamboat, huh?"

Justin giggled, and then with a smile said, "Seriously, go!"

I shook my head, shaking all the sleep out, "Alright, love ya, Justin." He nodded.

I slunk out the window without any troubles. I just missed Ken coming in and repeating his statement. I ran to the gas station near Owen's house and paused briefly.

Owen was there, filling his pick-up with gas. I stared at him like a doe stares at oncoming headlights. Then, after 30 seconds I briskly started walking.

The gas station attendant was in sight, so Owen had a casual air about him that made me feel like a foul odor was moving around us. So I oddly kept my nose in folds on my face sucking my bottom lip in to block my nostrils.

"Hey, kiddo, have fun?"

I looked up at him, smiled, and left.

Doing that, and nothing more, not even a nod, was a suicide wish when he was putting on an act. I knew I was supposed to make this charade of a good relationship between us as believable as possible and instead I said nothing, in front of a few townspeople.

So, in short, and not to go into any further detail

that I prefer to suppress, Owen had progressed on his beatings.

I think I finally figured him out. It's basically as if he's a moth and my pain is a light. He's attracted to pain, maybe even just my pain; I wasn't sure.

It wasn't like a sexual perversion either, it was more like there were bits of machinery guiding his actions, including the hate in his eyes and the wicked smile he adhered to.

The one thing he did the most was changing tactics. He liked to see me scream, bruise, bleed, and even just watching me curl up in a silenced pain amused him.

And even when I had no reaction (which honestly with proof of memory I can only say it happened once) he still liked to hurt me.

How do I know this? I study myself, and my life, and **I watch him**.

Most people would close their eyes; I'm sure, because that's what my body naturally wants to do. Eric said that would help.

But I wanted to be sure of something. I wanted to see if Owen ever felt slightly bad at all for what he did to me. Maybe he had more human in him than I was aware of. Maybe there was hope. After all, he was human enough to create excuses.

He came up with pretexts like, "I told you to stay out of my den," or the even less believable: "What are you eating?" He'd kick me down in my hollow stomach, "That's my food; go buy your own."

First of all, he didn't give me money and I was a small child, unable to get a job yet. How was I supposed to buy anything? Second, who deserved to be beaten when they ate the food from their own residential area?

161

Owen simply had a pain fixation. I watched his face and kept my eyes open. His eyes always held that same gleam of brutality. Not once was there a break in the sadism.

I still went to school every day and things actually began to get better. After time, the bruise on my neck faded (though the scarring from the burns did not). My neck stopped hurting altogether by the end of that summer before first grade.

My hoodie was outgrown quickly, and long before that, I threw it out. This merely resulted in people seeing the subtle bruises and my complete unpopularity.

As discouraging as it was, Justin was right. It was obvious that some human was harming me. Yet, everyone seemed to be conveniently oblivious. Nobody in the town wanted a thing to do with any situation as obviously wretched and law-involving as mine.

Eric, Justin and I met up at the Diner and walked to school together every day.

After school I spent time by myself more often than not. Eric and Justin were good company, but sometimes I lacked the enthusiasm to have fun with them.

Ironically, in April of 2143 (toward the end of our first grade school year) I started seeing some more of April... the girl who barely ever talked.

Our first meeting happened on accident, as most situations of irony do. I was sitting in my tree house, day after day as the norm of my recent life dictated.

April emerged from the natural dusty fog that the unseen animals in the forest made when they ran in bushes looking for mates or bringing food to mates they'd already found.

162

Well, that was the excuse I made for the dust anyway. There may have been several other reasons.

Anyway:

April had several things in hand usually. She carried a small easel and professional looking canvases, and of course, her tool belt of paintbrushes.

The third time I caught her painting in the woods, my curiosity got the best of me. I couldn't believe that she hadn't seen me watching her yet.

(... not that I meant to watch her by any means, but it was impossible not to with her always appearing at the most random times...)

I jumped off of my tree house, skipping the pitiful ladder and landing in the pine needles on a knee and a shoe.

I was only an inch from the six-year-old April, but she was unstirred. For some reason, that startled me and I fell back onto my rump.

She looked at me and scowled, "Don't you have somewhere else to be?"

I just looked at her, unblinkingly, and she continued to glare.

"What are you painting?" I asked to "break the ice".

Her look somewhat softened and she turned her canvas around.

I expected to see a good painting, but what I saw didn't appeal to me at all. Instead of saying anything bad about it though, I asked, "What is it?"

April gasped, "Hmpf! As if you could paint better!"

I frowned. I hadn't even spoken my mind. What I said wasn't insulting. Either April could read minds or she was self-conscious and dumb.

"Hey, I just can't see it for what it is, I guess."

From my small experience in a small-town school with short group interactions, I figured out that if you are humble and sometimes self-insulting, people with low self-esteem will respond better to you. For some reason it makes them feel better, as if you're confirming to them that not everyone in the world is perfect.

Back then, I thought I was absolutely white-as-snow, heaven-sent, angel-perfect material. My philosophy in first grade became one of self-encouragement: that obviously I was the good guy in a real live epic novel and Owen would be defeated by me one day.

April responded almost as I expected her to, "It's a tree," she said, shortly, and turned around and walked away.

I frowned, and followed her.

After a few yards back toward the town, April turned around and yelled at me, "What the heck do you want, 'Mrs. Shutter'?"

She threw me for a loop, but it only took a moment for the last name to register,

"What, like Sheriff Shutter?"

My first stupid thought was that she hated the Sheriff as much as the rest of us and was just trying to insult me, for reasons I was still oblivious to.

I was in first grade and being the little oddball that I was, I didn't have any "crushes", so the following seemed preposterous to me:

"Don't play dumb. I know you and Eric are going out. You've been with him since Kindergarten, when everybody knew I liked him! Why would you do that?"

"Woah!" This explained a lot, but what a pathetic excuse to hate someone as wonderful as I was,

"Oh, please!" I thought as she started crying. What a little pansy. She was crying over Eric when she never even talked to him. She wasn't even close to him.

"Okay, listen, kid." I said, turning off my normal child voice, "I don't even like Eric 'like that'. We are and will always be friends. And you? You are an interesting lady, but you're stupid. If you like Eric so much, then talk to him. Don't cry to me about it, you little..."

I'd never been punched by a girl before... Or anyone but Owen for that matter. I called her a name that Owen called me several times.

"You 'little bitch', come back here," he'd say, "You stupid 'little bitch', just die."

Of course, I didn't mean it as harshly as Owen had, and I didn't actually mean to say it in the first place. It was just something that sort-of slipped out.

April gave me a black eye, and when I didn't cry, she didn't say she was sorry. And when she didn't stop crying, even though she had a tough-butt punch that I respected, I didn't apologize either.

We both had hilarious negative opinions of each other. So, us two little girls, both unwilling to get up at the moment just sat in the pine needles and listened to her puny little sobs.

When she finally settled down, she said, "You know, I'm not sorry."

"Makes two of us," I said.

165

I noticed that horrible anger that I usually buried had surfaced without warning in my voice. I quickly justified it in my thoughts, "I have enough damn bruising and my wounds don't heal all the way anymore..."

*April paused, standing up and pivoting her left foot at the toe, back and forth, "But I **am embarrassed**..."*

"So?" I looked up, glaring at her.

"Well, you deserved what you got. You shouldn't call a woman that. It's demeaning."

Her vocabulary startled me. I didn't know that latter word. Eric hadn't even used it. Ever.

I wasn't about to admit to that though, so I just retorted, "You're not a woman, little girl."

April bit her lip and scowled at me in frustration, "Boy, you just don't even give people time to talk. See. This is why I don't talk to people. They don't want to listen."

I paused, "... I'm sorry I didn't listen." I said: making sure she knew I still wasn't sorry for anything else. Mainly because I still thought she was a wuss.

"I'm embarrassed because I know you're right. I should talk to Eric, but I'm nervous as well. He doesn't even notice me when you're around. And we never talk anymore."

"You two used to talk?"

"Oh, well... no. Not really. Well, yes. He was there when my family came to town in the summer before kindergarten and I said hello and he said hi back."

I rolled my eyes.

April was a pretty little girl, but she had a way of making herself look homely. Her skin was darker than mine by two shades at least (which wasn't a big deal,

166

because [like my parents] I was border-line albino). She had short blackish-brown hair that she always had tied in a bun and huge, dark brown eyes.

She would've looked like Snow White if she'd tidy up. Her eyebrows were furrowed, unlike how she normally had them relaxed, and I was guessing that when she got older they'd look a little less like caterpillars.

"Okay..." I said, after we were both silent for a while. "So, I was right, and you are understanding things... um, what do you want?"

"Shouldn't I be the one asking that? Art critic." She teased and poked her tongue out at me.

"No. I always hang around here. It's my sanctuary. You and a little girl named Miranda have now both bothered me."

"Hey! Wait a minute! The forest isn't owned by you! Anybody can walk on in here."

I shivered after hearing "anybody", thinking of Owen.

"And besides," She continued, "You were the one who jumped in on my peaceful walk."

... Well, she had me there. I wasn't going to be stubborn anymore, and the oddest thing happened.

I felt like helping April out.

"April..." I started, and paused, looking at her concerned face, "Do you actually have any friends?"

She frowned again, making herself look all fuzzy in the forehead region again, "What's that supposed to mean?"

"It means what it means!" I said, "What's not to get? It's a simple question."

167

"Well, there's a quote that says, 'sisters are god's pick of life-long friends'. And I've got sisters..."

I laughed a little, "Well, there's another thing I wouldn't know about... but I do know about Eric. I'd like to help you become his friend. The "and more" part will just fit in there, if you really like him that much."

"Really?!" April said, smiling.

There she was. There was the beautiful April who smiled without her teeth showing.

"Well yeah. I don't lie."

That was mostly true.

"Well, but why?"

"Because lying is stupid, it just gets you..."

April rolled her eyes, "No. Why do you want to help me, Joslin?"

"Well, duh, because you've proven yourself to be pretty cool. And you care about Eric so much, and so do I. That's why I think I should get the two of you together."

April smiled.

I scoffed, "Though I really don't see the point... We're in first grade. There's no reason to have a boyfriend."

"Oh, whatever, you silly girl." April said, "I'm going to go back home before it gets dark, you wanna join me? ...oh wait..."

April said "oh wait" because of my eye, of course. I stood silent, busy contemplating whether I wanted a beating tonight and tomorrow, or nothing tonight and have a near death experience when I returned to Owen.

I made my decision. Owen didn't scare me.

"April, no worries, I'm really clumsy, we can tell 'em I fell."

"You're not clumsy! You liar. You told me you didn't lie!" She laughed, "I saw you land perfectly, jumping out of that tall tree!"

"It was lucky," I said, pulling up my pant leg and showing her the giant scar that Owen gave me, which looked kind of like the scar Justin had from falling off his bike last summer.

April said, "Well, even if you are clumsy," Her eyes shifted from my scar to my eyes, "I'm not comfortable with lying to my folks. We could just wait until that's gone for you to sleep over..."

I had a bad flashback when she said that...

"You're not going out in public until that particular bruise is gone," Owen laughed in my mind. I patted my neck.

April wasn't going to interfere with my plans. I wanted to do what I wanted to do! I deserved some bits of happiness in my little life!

"Hey, you won't have to lie." I said, "If they even bring it up, I'll tell them I deserved it."

April wasn't satisfied, I could tell, but I'd made up my mind that I wasn't going home, and I was curious to learn more about someone who wasn't an only child. She seemed to be the only one here (in Tip Sod) who fit that category.

I looked at her with a plea in my eyes, and she said, "Oh, alright, but if I get in trouble, you're outta there."

"Oh please," I said, "Like you're even a troublemaker."

April looked back at me as she walked forward. Her smirk was very innocent and only confirmed my notion. Her big deep-brown eyes glinted with dark green speckles in the light.

She turned back, and we both ran out of the forest. We emerged in Tip Sod at the back of this old building that was across from the jailhouse. We walked to the front and I paused while April kept walking ahead.

There was a metal sign on hinges above the doorway that said, "Tipsod Station". Then on the building, was paint—only slightly chipped, which said, "Tip Sod Storage".

Along with those signs was an old wooden sign leaning up against the side of the building that said, "The snack shack" with a picture of a dolphin by the last "k" for some reason.

April called out to me, "Hurry up!"

"Hey. April!" I said, as she ran back over to me, "You're a painter, right? You could re-paint that sign. Make it look all pretty again." I indulged her.

She smiled big (still not showing any teeth) "Well sure, if I don't get grounded for comin' back after dark! Now, hurry up!"

I followed as she ran to the jailhouse, and turned into the same tunnel that Eric, Justin and I went through to get to Eric's house.

I kept walking through the tunnel even in my confusion, when April stopped midway at the dim light to the right side.

I realized suddenly that there was a door that I never saw on the right side of the tunnel. April pulled a chain string that was flowing from a hole in the wall, and I heard a little bell ring.

"Elves..." I muttered.

"Huh?" said April.

"Huh?" I said back, making myself laugh.

April just smiled again.

Then, the door opened, and I gasped.

Aina Tilda, my mother, stood on the other side of the door.

Chapter 4: Changes

Joslin's black hair mingles with the algae in the lake water to the side of the vast mansion field that Miranda lived in. She didn't know her history of American government too well, but she did pay attention to the more recent events.

More than twenty years ago, just a few years before Joslin was born, President Mclaiden created a different kind of atmosphere in the United States. She was a radical "white" Amish woman who believed that a greener America was a better America.

Of course, as previously mentioned, she had her insane kinks that caused her own downfall, but there were many people who loved her "Saving Mother Earth" campaigns.

She's the reason there are "mansion fields" in the first place. Miranda lives in one.

Original mansion fields were produced from well-preserved "scrap wood" (or metal or other sturdy materials) that had been recycled. Only items that environmentalists and aristocrats both agreed were worthy were allowed within construction zones.

The construction zones were old-fashioned by law. Mclaiden banned any "harmful mechanics" and in order to make her plan more economically friendly for the builders and the state. The fact that all of the houses were handmade and still so elaborate made them way too expensive for Joslin's taste.

The fad of these fields became outdated after her short two-year term in office, but a few of them were still being created. Miranda's house is the newest in the neighborhood, and the mansion **field** itself is relatively new too—it hadn't been there when they were younger.

Cars are parked in small storage garages up at the top of the hill. The owners can walk down the hill on stone paths to get to their scattered houses in the clearing.

It's an artistic way to live, very different from rural, suburban, or city life, in that they have no street address. If they want mail, they'd get it at the post office by signing in for a P.O. Box.

Miranda enjoys this style of life very much, but mostly because of the fact that she's had very few building restrictions. She owns her own property, and can add in close to three miles of extra rooms if she ever wants to. There are about five other houses in the field as far as Joslin knows, all quite far away from one another.

The small lake that she sits in is probably a mile and a half away, but Miranda's house is closer to the thick edges of the forest than any of the other houses in the field. Within the outer trees and leafy growth sits this little water-hole.

Joslin slept yet again. It's all she can do until she musters up the courage to visit people from her past, and walk into the town.

Miranda is the only person she came into contact with after all those years of exile.

She wants to see her other friends desperately, but she didn't dare go into town, and for the past few weeks. All the time Joslin stayed with Miranda thus-far, she either helped her unpack boxes of her endless supply of things, or Miranda had gone into town for a date. So during those times, Joslin explored the house and the woods.

Joslin spends time in this moment in particular remembering and waiting and trying desperately to keep herself calm while her thoughts stir. *It's dangerous for me to be roused... I am... inhuman... I thought with a smile, as I lifted my translucent hands. The algae slithered from my palm back into the water.*
■■

I looked up at my mother, then blinked my eyes, and saw the features change slightly.

April's mother had short black hair, a flat nose, and beautiful dark brown eyes. Somehow, the differences seemed slight in the moment and I had to flutter my eyes every few seconds to make my mother's face go away.

At least, that was until she spoke, "April Raina RAPID!" She yelled, "Did you hit again!?"

April's lip started to tremble. The yelling itself didn't stir me, but the source did. I'd never heard a woman yell like that.

So I paused for a moment, but remembering my promise to April, I broke the tension and said, "Well, I deserved it. I called her a bih—a naughty word..."

April's mother seemed unmoved, but she

straightened her lips and stopped frowning at us.

"Well, for heaven's sake, get in here. You're going to catch a cold."

The evening air in Tip Sod town had subjective properties involving heat. The only time that any cold air broke through the thick layer of condescending warmth was in the months of December and January or during rainstorms.

It wasn't raining, and we were in mid-April. There was no way in hell we'd catch a cold. Apparently, April's mother was unaware of this truth, and I let it slide because she didn't appear like she was a woman to be trifled with.

"Dan!" April's mother yelled. "Get down here and look at what your daughter did!"

"Thud, thud, thud," said the stair steps, under the weight of this man.

When I heard the footsteps, I expected to see an insanely fat man, but what I saw was what appeared to be a body builder from a show Eric's grandpa would watch.

April was shaking, and rightfully so, but what she muttered sounded like it involved irritation, not fear, "He better not spank me in front of a friend."

Dan was wearing construction worker's smock and had one foot in a boot, and the other in just a sock.

"What?" He said goofily. His voice was deep, and yet still much lighter than I expected.

April's mother pointed at my face, and April's father snorted, which caused April's mother to glare, which caused Dan to stifle his laugh.

His voice was serious, but light-hearted, "April,

175

why did you punch this girl?"

"She called me a name! A bad one. But she's a friend, so you don't need to make a big fuss and talk to her parents or nothin'" said April.

"I'll decide that, now you come here, young lady." said Dan, his face still humored, and his voice feigning a sort of sternness.

"Dear," April's mother said, gesturing me, "Why don't you come over here, and we'll put some ice on that."

I grabbed at her outstretched hand and said, "It's Joslin..." as we walked into the kitchen.

I wasn't nervous about anything. My spirits were much too high for any fuss or worry. I was in a family environment at last!

As we walked into the kitchen, I noticed another person coming down the stairs and into the living room. She looked exactly like April, but older.

"That must be a sister."

"Oh, yeah, that's Autumn, my second. Are you and April close, sweetie?"

*"Well, we **are** friends." I said. And my name is Joslin... I thought.*

*Pet names drove me mad. Although my parents **did** use them, they named me Joslin legally, and I strongly felt that adults were supposed to use my name when speaking to me.*

It was odd to me that an adult wanted to know "soft" information about me...

Are you and April close?

"Soft" as in: not of dire importance or dark

circumstance.

She was just a mom, asking a question.

I smiled.

*"I think we are going to be **good** friends!" I said, optimistically.*

April's mother beamed brightly, and the night went on. Rooms filled with laughter, yelling, personal jokes, card games, winning, TV watching, poking fun, whining, and giggling.

April had six sisters, but I only met three, two of which were unable to talk to me, as they were both under two-years-old. Her oldest sister no longer lived with the family, and Autumn was too old to go to any functions that the school held. She was almost nineteen and trying desperately to get out of town. April's other two sisters were in middle school and they were off on a field trip to some kind of big capitol city.

Dan, April, and I played a game of War, while Autumn and April's mother played Speed about a hundred times.

With watchful brown eyes, the clock was stalked, and April's mother called out, "Alright! Bedtime for the little bees that have got school in the morning! It's a Thursday night, and you two may see each other again on the weekend!"

April nudged me, "Hey, we can just pal around in my room, come on!" She grinned, this time showing her ridiculously crooked teeth.

"Woah ho, ho-no. Ms. Joslin is sleeping right here on our comfy sofa tonight. Early morning rise n' shine comin' up, I don't want any excuses."

April and I both pouted, but did as we were told. I giggled, and adjusted myself nicely on the couch.

Autumn ruffled my hair, "Nice to meet you."

"Likewise." I said, straight and emotionless. Autumn never seemed to show emotion, so I had a hard time showing any back.

Anyway, I laid there on the couch, and April's mother kissed my forehead, and tucked me in with a fluffy throw blanket. I had two slow and warm tears seep from my eyes over that moment, and my throat was a little choked up from how much I missed my parents.

But soon, the lights were off, and I quietly drifted...

■■■

Long ago, outside of Joslin's memory, she was sleeping soundly on the couch in April Rapid's living room. Water tapped it's fingernails at the window earnestly, and streams hissed music into the drains of Tip Sod Town. The rain sounded off without notice; the entire town slept soundly.

She'd written off another discovery about herself on the day she heard the rattling in Owen's house.

The tharpels' curiosity distracted them from hiding their abilities to heal.

They knew what was in the fifth room. They wanted to let her know more than anything.

Suddenly as Joslin was sleeping peacefully, her humanity diminished. She dreamed unaware that her entire body was gleaming with that cream-colored light.

In her sleep, her breath stopped instantaneously. Her body made no movements, and her heart ceased to pulse.

Across town, in a tattered armchair in the small black oak house, Owen Tilda woke with a start. He ran to Joslin's room and prepared for anything his imagination could come up with. Like any normal night, Joslin was not to be found in her bed.

Owen, however, never noticing how often this truly happened, became suspicious. He lurched into the hallway, like a monster lurching through a marsh, and he crept into the fifth room silently.

The only thing Owen paid any mind to was a drawstring connected to an attic door on the ceiling near the entryway. He pulled the drawstring, as he had before, and climbed a pull-out staircase.

Shoving boxes carelessly, he looked upon the grinning cream-colored light emanating from within one of the boxes. And *he* grinned, sighed with relief, and then slowly stepped out. And as he did, the glow continued, transferring from Joslin in tufts to the mysterious source in the attic of the black oak house on the other side of the dead-end highway.

And Joslin's body dropped without a sound from its floating position. She breathed, and tossed and turned, like a little girl would as she sleeps through the night at a good friend's house. Ever unaware, her life continued as if she were truly human.

Now, in the present, sitting in her newly-furnished room, Joslin continues to write about her life in that brown journal. Joslin has a *true* story to write, and a perfect place to write it in.

The next morning, I woke up earlier than everyone else. I walked into the bathroom and saw my eye had healed.

April's father got up before I left the house. I don't remember why I left so early. I guess I didn't want to wake April up before she had to.

Dan said, "That shiner sure took its time dimming down." He said sarcastically, "Can't even tell it was there."

I shrugged, "I'm a fast healer."

Dan looked at me with suspicion, "I'll say. Well, April couldn'a hit ya too hard. You wanna wait around a while, we'll make you some breakfast."

"Nah, I'm good, tell April I'll see 'er at school, okay?" I said with a smile.

Dan smirked.

Nothing else happened.

That night I returned to the black oak house and Owen actually avoided me. I didn't know why...

I actually forgot most of my 2nd grade experience. All I remember, in fact, was my ambition to follow through with helping April on her valiant quest to win the heart of Eric Shutter. I remember the hilarious frustration we both experienced when the natural course of life events played out. Eric was so close to her, but just oh, so far away, too.

What I mean is: Eric was physically hanging around April all the time. After school, and during breaks and weekends...

"And, uh, hand me that screw driver over there, would ya, boy?"

You see, Eric loved to create things, and as an aspiring carpenter, the occupational construction worker—Dan Rapid—was an exceptional teacher for him.

"Sure thing, Mr. Rapid," said Eric, running to get the tools that sat on the desk in the corner where April and I stood.

I quickly handed the screw driver to April, who nervously hid it behind her back, because she had no idea what I was doing. Or what **she** was doing for that matter—hah!

I nonchalantly practiced yo-yo tricks, on the side wall of the garage as Eric approached us.

"I knew I just saw it here!" he said, looking sternly at the desk.

"Oh. Uh. Here, Eric. I have this, I think..."

April managed to get out some words which made me believe that she meant to say, "I think I have what you're looking for here, Eric," but she froze. It was a miracle she got words out of her mouth at all.

"Um. Thanks. Uh... Alice." Eric said, and then ran back to April's father.

I stopped my yo-yo-fun-times, because April's face was as red as an Irish man's back after a tropical vacation.

She immediately dashed off into the woods,

screaming and wailing like a big, fat baby.

I slowly followed her, and Eric seriously did not help my cause by calling out, "Hey, Jos, you leaving?"

"I'll be back, Eric." I said between my teeth.

It was really frustrating having April suddenly so close to me and having to deal with her easily swaying emotions.

I met up with April under the tree house which used to be my sanctuary.

*"All he cares about is **you**."*

I expected as much...

"April, I'm working the best I can here, but you're the one who actually has to get up the courage to talk to him."

She looked at me, beneath her tears, and nodded softly. Despite her quick assumptions, and reactions, she learned quickly afterwards, and her spirits lifted very easily.

*All of her sisters, aside from the eldest, (whose name actually **was** Alice) acted just like this.*

I held April's hand and she talked to me as we walked back.

"You know," she said, "Normally, after my father's done with a carpentry project he lets me paint it."

"Oh yeah?"

"So, I was thinking, that I could ask him to paint it, in front of Eric. Paint the whatever-it'll-be. And he'll finally notice me."

"That's... as good of a plan as any... definitely worth a shot."

So, the plan was initiated. About five days later, Eric Shutter, Dan Rapid, and I watched as a seven-year-old painted a masterpiece on this road-racer-go-kart.

It was—so far—the best thing April had ever painted. And on that day, Eric definitely noticed her, and from then on, he remembered her name.

I never discovered anything more that bound them together, or any evidence that they became good friends, but April seemed happy. She left the subject alone, and so did I.

Thus, I supposed I'd accomplished the mission. Or rather she did, with surprisingly little help from me.

And that's all I can recall from 2nd grade.

In the summer after second grade (before 3rd) I was eight, and so was April, and my long lost friend Miranda emerged once more.

"Long lost friend" of course is a drool of sarcasm.

Miranda and I only became friends for one reason, just one, and this friendship didn't come about until the school year started.

In the meantime, during the stretch of summertime days, I hung out with Eric and Justin like normal, until one day, April returned to my life to invite me to dance classes.

Immediately, without thought, I yelled out, "Yes!"

Then she handed me a leotard, tights, and some ballet slippers.

I'd been rather gawky-looking up until this point. My wardrobe consisted of random things I'd picked out with Owen at Wal-mart.

The drives into civilization, by the way, were horrendously silent. I mean... I pretended to hear the grass talking to me just to keep company. Owen didn't even listen to music, to my knowledge.

He always bought me collared shirts from the little boys' section (which I picked out), and I kept the buttons buttoned to the top.

The scarring on my neck still peeked above the collar, but people just thought I was a nerd with a collared shirt and a rash from itching at scratchy material.

Long story short—our ballet teacher was the old teacher from kindergarten, the one that I hated—April saw my scarring along with several other silently staring little girls. The teacher just told me to put a jacket on and leave to get parental consent, but handed me no form. She could barely even look at me.

April exited the school's gym room (which served as a dance studio during the summer) and told me that the teacher told her to never bring me back there again.

She didn't ask me about the scarring. She just hugged me, and we stood there, and I tried not to cry but I whimpered... Tears never spilled in front of April though, I made sure of that. The tolerance was tough, but I was tough, so I convinced myself that it was easy to hold up in front of her.

I let go of the hug, and smiled at April, "Hey, as if I need anyone to teach me how ta dance!" and I spun around very clumsily, then once more quite gracefully.

She laughed very lightly and linked arms with me, "Hey, why don't we go to my house for a REAL sleepover?"

"What about class? ..."

April shook her head, "Any lady acting like that... For one, she's not a lady (correcting myself). Two: she's not a good teacher. All of those little girls... the ones who chose to stay and not walk out on her, they're learning how to outcast. I personally would rather be exiled than join them."

That night ended with her and me laughing and dancing ourselves to sleep.

We showed them!

April was definitely my ally.

The school year started, and our small classes doubled in size with about 20 students instead of fewer than 10. I actually appreciated our third grade teachers. Our school had been recognized. We existed to the world at last, or at least Alabama knew we existed.

So, to populate our area a little more, they had willing substitute staff members of a school district about 50 miles away make a commute to Tip Sod every other week to teach classes. This was very odd but good, because up until that point, children moving up into high school had to be home schooled or transfer schools.

In my third grade classes, I was a pretty hated kid. I didn't care much because I was treated the same no matter where I went.

I took fifth grade math with Miranda. She was the only one who befriended me in that grade level.

Our first impressions of each other (way back when) weren't good, but our meeting was brief. When we started talking in her fifth grade class, she had an explosively social, but soft personality.

She always talked about the two cultures she embraced: the Ojibwan tribe of her mother's ancestry, and a bastardy Spanish-African father created a very enthusiastic mixed-American out of Miranda.

She talked about church like she hated it. She said that Pastor Lance preached a bunch of lies, and that he *was stupid.*

She, unlike Eric, didn't poke fun at the Christian-Lutheran religion that most of our town practiced. She scorned it and insulted the foundations of the beliefs. She was determined to constantly communicate about how right she was if ever the topic of religion was brought up.

I was unsure of whether God existed or not, but I was pretty sure that he or she did. I didn't really care what form that being was in either. However... my parents were Christian, so her ignorance bothered and insulted me.

Miranda would always mutter prayers to Orishas, and talk about scenery, calling it "Mother Earth". Her beliefs interested me, but I never wanted to get into the details with her, because I was sure it would lead to some Christ-bashing talk.

Anyway, the fun times in math class came from our talks about some of the boys in the class.

*By this point, I began to realize that I was attracted to some of them, and then when I said something to Miranda, she told me, "Well, **I've** already **kissed** a boy!"*

She said that if I ever felt like kissing somebody, I should just do it.

*"Boys think they don't like kisses, but they **so** do. You give him a peck on the lips and he'll be blushing, and happy."*

I thought some of these boys were very cute, so I could've followed Miranda's advice. I was a stubborn, perfect, strong, and tough little thing (in my mind). Yet the idea of kissing a boy made me super shy.

The action was foreign, and seemed rather useless, so I quickly let my hopes of kisses go. Ever since I brought the subject up, Miranda continued to bring it up. I just smiled and laughed with her.

Unfortunately, my shy behavior wasn't the only thing preventing me from having a crush. Boys were just mean in fifth grade. I was a puny little third grader, who just happened to carry a fifth grade math book. Boys pushed me around and down and treated me like crap most of the time.

"Because I haven't had enough of this at home..." I thought sarcastically.

With my lame wardrobe, I didn't look appealing anyway. I just mainly tried to stay out of the way of these boys who pushed me around. Miranda watched them push me down the stairs, and shove me into walls and did nothing. She even had the nerve to talk to me afterwards as if nothing had happened.

Well, the saying goes, "If life gives you lemons, make lemonade." I had two lemons at that point: the older boys and secrets about Owen, my lemonade was truth—something like that. I'm terrible at metaphors.

I added to the saying, convincing myself that some sort of action needed to take place. Some sort of clemency for what I've been through.

I repeated to myself softly on my walks home, "Life gives me lemons; I'll make lemonade, and guzzle it down. With blood, sweat, and tears, I'll make the most amazing lemonade ever... then drink it up and happily sigh..."

April thought that my addition to the phrase was disgusting. "Lemonade with blood in it?" she scrunched her face up, "eww... creepy..."

April was also my only ally who didn't know about Owen and my excuse for any bruises was that I tripped down the stairs too much. With fifth graders pushing me down the stairs, that was true, and so what April didn't know didn't make me feel guilty.

Also, like I said, she never asked about my neck scars. April was very respectful of my boundaries and any boundaries in general. She never asked me to tell her anything that I didn't speak of on my own. She listened, and she talked, but never pried.

My train of thought switched tracks constantly, and April also tolerated that. She walked home with me almost every day after school, stopping at the gas station because she was afraid of the highway.

Justin and Eric seemed to keep well to themselves even through November. We'd hang out on the weekends, but that was about it, usually.

Miranda wasn't an ally at all—just an amusement of a friend. She hardly ever shut-up to let me talk and she only cared about herself. So I shrugged and listened, knowing I'd never want to hang out with her outside of school. Truly though, April and Miranda were just brief encounters in my life.
▪▪

Joslin laughs as she writes that last sentence, and then pauses to get a peanut butter and jelly sandwich and a drink.

She runs up the spiral steps in Miranda's house, and right into the kitchen. Most of the boxes were out of the way now, and the living room had dozens of dream catchers hanging from the ceiling...

"Brief encounters" is what Joslin wrote. And of course, it's ironic. Miranda certainly wasn't and isn't her favorite person in the world. Yet, Joslin compiles a snack in *Miranda's* kitchen. Of all the places she could*'ve lived in, this was the most unusual.*

As Joslin sets her bread out and grabs the peanut butter, the front door swings open and Miranda runs into the house.

"Joslin, why don't you let me take you out on the town?" She says, poking her smiley face into the kitchen.

Without her consent, Miranda grabs Joslin's arm and pulls her outside of the house, and the locket on Joslin's chest starts throbbing with her own heartbeat.

To me, although it may be wrong, the most important moment in Tip Sod happened as I opened the fifth door on the 2nd floor of the black oak house. This moment had been secretly anticipated for almost three years and finally, at age eight, I was able to quench my thirst for this unsolved mystery.

I gulped, and opened the door swiftly, and started to sprint into the room when a huge gust of wind poured out through a side window.

The light that previously poured into the hallway from the crack under the door had come from a bulb. The bulb connected to a rusty socket on the wall to my left near the ceiling. It had dimmed since last I saw it, and now flickered wildly.

The greenhouse styled window on the side of the room still had its rims, but the glass had spilled everywhere. This was to the fault of a tree from the back wood; it had grown so close and big that it had broken in with its branches. They transformed into cold, brittle limbs inside of the house.

I ran to the window, angrily looking for a way to

189

stifle the sound and halt the bombardment of the wind. My efforts in vain, the wind shrieked an unmerciful cry which killed my curious mood and broke me down into a sobbing girl, curled up on the hard wood floor.

Strong winds blew through my backyard back in Iowa as well... I could feel Aina and Talib again. Still after three years I cringed. I had grown to hate wind due to the memories of the day when my parents lay dead. The wind tonight was as constricting to my thoughts as Owen's frigid grip on my body.

Alabama was mostly warm, but during these later months of the year, namely December for this moment, the winds became something I abhorred more than anything. They carried with them a chill, and swerved into my head in that moment and I felt like I was about to explode. I fought against the gust and stood in the corner of the room, shivering just to shake the feeling.

Then, I looked around. The room was completely empty except for cobwebs and dust balls. On the wall furthest from the door the large-scale greenhouse styled window framed the room, and bubbled into trees of the forest. It almost replaced the middle of the wall completely.

I looked up to see what the ceiling looked like and there was a door... Who would've guessed that a door would be on the ceiling?

It even looked just like an average front door for a house would look. It made me happier than most things could make me because it was the brightest and happiest thing I saw in Owen's house.

The reason that the door was so wonderful was the fact that it wasn't composed of black oak, which was Owen's favorite building material apparently. At least, I figured as much, since he structured his entire house out of it.

The door was a cherry wood, which was found in my home in Iowa on the counters. (Truthfully, I believed my vision of the door to be a hallucination, just because I couldn't gather it to be real.)

I got a small exercise trampoline that used to be under all the toys in the toy room before I cleaned up. I bounced up and grabbed the golden latch handle hanging off of the door.

The door looked bleak, as it had been, and I realized that I was, in fact, hallucinating about my parent's front door when I first looked up at it. Still, the door existed in the first place, and it still intrigued me.

When the door opened, a roll-up ladder with a bunch of grime and sawdust came down. I felt myself smile in wonder as the dust peppered my face. The attic seemed to be nothing but a force that beckoned me.

I hadn't smiled like that in a while, and I couldn't help it and I had no clue as to why.

I climbed the ladder and everything in the space above the door was pitch-black. Back down the ladder... I went to get a candle from my room. I lit it with matches from the downstairs cupboards. I tiptoed as I passed so I wouldn't wake Owen, who had fallen asleep with his bald head peeking out at me over his chair.

I climbed up again.

I walked through several boxes with random stuff in them that was not of my concern. There was a light flickering in the room aside from my candle, so I pushed myself toward it; the adrenaline rushed through my head.

Somehow, this endeavor felt even more dangerous than insulting Owen, or even returning to him after a break. My curiosity drove into me with determination. The room felt forbidden, but I kept moving the cobwebs until they were all out of my way and I pushed past the boxes and... my candle blew out.

Coming from, or near a small box in the corner was the consistent glow that filled my gaze. I felt my heart skip five beats that I counted in my head. I was filled with awe and then I opened the cover to the box.

My brain stopped chiming; my lungs ballooned as I gasped. I felt a horror engulf my entire body, which stood there, knees locked, throat dry, eyes frozen. I stood two levels above a murderer's sleeping head.

I lifted my mother's locket out of the box.

Chapter 5: Escape

I held my breath, afraid to breathe momentarily. The familiar orange glow had turned into an eerie yellow as soon as I picked it up, right when my fear escalated. Then as I continued holding my breath, the light vanished altogether, and the locket shook ferociously in my hand.

My body started glowing outwardly from the neck. I felt a pulse go through my already pulsing palm. It shot through my entire body like a mental atom bomb had just slid into me and exploded.

Memories that I didn't even know I had triggered off through my mind.

"God! No! Don't hurt my baby!" mother screamed.

"Please, leave us alone, take what you want, just leave us!" My dad said after her.

The man's face was covered, was it Owen's? Were his despicable freezing hands the ones that were holding that gun? I examined the memory. I recognized his hands; I recognized his standing position.

As my eyes looked at the locket, my memory looked back at things that I couldn't previously recall. It was like I was watching an old scene playing from a movie I knew, but had forgotten.

As I breathed again, I noticed the locket glowing once more. Of course, I finally realized the magical properties of this locket. I didn't understand them completely, but I knew they were there.

Owen pointed the gun at my parents and my mother held me tight.

My father, the tall, thin, muscular man that he was, stood in front of my mother and me, like a loyal

193

bear guarding its family.

Owen moved in closer and whisked me away from my mother's grasp within two seconds. My father couldn't even blink.

My mother screamed, "No! Not Joslin! Why are you here for Joslin?"

My heart danced a little with the false closeness of my mother's voice, and then Owen's came like nails on a chalkboard.

"Shut-up, I'm not here for her" then he paused; "...but..." I felt the gun on my head.

I saw my mother cry and my father made that hurting face I saw on him when he told mom that grandpa died.

"Tell us what you want!" My father screamed as Owen pushed his whole hand that was free down on my head.

"You're the one blocking it." Owen said.

"Me..." said the woman as hot tears swelled through my eyes.

My mother never sounded so frightened in her life before this. When I got my first scrape was the closest, but this was at least ten times more petrified.

"No. Not exactly," came Owen's voice again. "That locket around your neck; that would suffice."

My father lost all fear and looked the man with the gun eye to eye, "No," he said. He said it it with all the certainty in the world.

It made me mad at the time, I remembered, my father put my life in danger for his gift to mother.

I heard a gun's shot,

"Have it your way."

Owen yanked my hair and head back with his greasy hands and then pushed my forehead into the wall.

After that, the next thing I remembered was waking up in the hospital. I tried my best to think.

I put the locket around my own neck and tried. The locket latched itself like a tick to my neck on the skin near my jugular vein. At that point I began to see images from an ominous point of view,

That gunshot must've been a warning shot, sort of like the warning of a rattler's tail. After Owen slammed me into the wall, he lunged after my mother, chasing her into the backyard.

Knowing my mother, it was no surprise to see her stumble several times. Owen caught her on the last fatal fall.

The viewpoint changed slightly, and I watched a bird's-eye's, flickering glimpse.

He took a knife from a side pocket on his belt loop and cut her into her stomach. Her cuts all healed radically. So, he continued to cut her, and during the attack, my father ran out, probably after making sure I was still alive and okay.

He was shot in the head almost immediately after exiting the house; his body took a few more steps and then rolled next to where his wife lay struggling to stop Owen's every move even while dying.

Everything ended for them; everything changed for me in a split second, when Owen stripped the locket from her chest.

My father's body stopped convulsing, and he let his eyes go blank when he saw my mother die.

That locket had kept her alive. Her salvation was his only possible murder weapon.

After he killed her, I saw the sick bastard, cut her and burn her with matches. The marks stayed, yes, she was dead for sure. He burned her chest, he burned her neck. The image speckled away, as if my mind's cable connection was lost.

Without preparation, the whole scene played in my head again as if it were a memory. Still, I wasn't seeing it from my point of view; it was a non-existent bystander. Nonetheless, it terrified me.

We knew all along, and we showed Joslin all that we'd seen.

Although we collectively form her every part and compose her nerves and organ of thought, we were able to keep our memories from her until the right moment.

"Owen" as the humans call him, had hunted us all down.

Long before the point of our conception into the Joslin, we'd claimed the locket on Aina's neck as our home.

The magic collected from spell casting absorbed a spiritual energy far older than any of us were. The power and security of the piece was comforting and uplifting.

The beauty welded into the charm makes our lives exciting and purposeful in new and fantastic ways (for we are children of curiosity).

So we moved into the locket once Talib finished creating it, and dwelled near Aina. The locket clung to her, the dying woman, and kept her sustained.

Talib forfeited his own immortality to preserve her. He would live only as long as she would live, and if the locket ever left her chest, her death was imminent.

She knew this though, so Aina kept the locket connected to her body at all times.

We dwelled there for hundreds of years, hesitating to leave the comfort.

However, Talib was such a good friend to us, and we were so thankful to him for keeping Aina alive in such a perfect way, we had to repay him somehow.

We knew their desires, and through the help of their passion and love, and of course half of their D. N. A. and spirit; we created the Joslin girl as a present that would last eternity.

As our human half lay unconscious on the floor while her parents were under attack, we separated, and our humanity dissipated. We tried to help, but we could do nothing. The one called "Owen" tore the locket from Aina's flesh.

The bullet in Talib's head would not have killed him if Owen had not stolen the locket...

We had to preserve our humanity. We had to heal.

Us and the locket necklace, we are the only remnants of the once immortal couple.

In an instant, I felt my body in the attic again. My heat escalated.

I breathed chaotically; my heart beat stomped and raced as my hand rested on a golden orb of flickering light. The locket slowly and surely settled into a calm and dim, but sick salmon color as I caught my breath and tried thinking calmly.

I had one gut instinct conjuring the single thought that played itself violently through my head like an advertising text display:

"Get out of the house, get out of the house—get out of the house, now."

Without thinking any longer, I began to slink toward the trap door. I walked onto the roll-out ladder and blew out my candle. The smoke danced lightly through the darkened air, contradicting my mood entirely. Whispers seemed to cling in ashes around the missing fire.

Step by step my feet dropped stiffly on the ladder. It wobbled and shifted and I became as frightened as a small puppy. My teeth began to chatter along with the clinking of the steps.

I left the trampoline in there and ran to my room. I packed all my things. My father's notebook and some Disney DVD's found their place in my bag. I packed two changes of clothing and the canned food that I stole from the pathetic canned food drive at our school.

(I actually don't feel bad about that; it was "food for the hungry" after all).

My final act of business in that dusty place was to lay the roses on the ground as they were before. I saw it as a routine and traditional ritual.

For Eric spoke briefly once of the little girls who lived here and how they all disappeared.

"Yeah, Owen's had a few kids adopted, but they all left. I think most of them are way older now. Like in their teens... if they're still ALIVE!"

I never heard any full story about them, and noted his tale as a harmless rumor.

But, say they were real:

Maybe it was a tradition for them to leave roses lying on the floor like I found them before... Maybe they all escaped his clutches, as I promised myself to do then.

I tiptoed down the flight as quietly as possible. I can't explain why or how, but it's almost as if the locket helped my feet be quieter. It helped me have patience with the creaking door that quieted if one moved it *slowly. The necklace was like breath supply for my staggering heart.*

*I believe it was reminding me, "She **died** for you, so don't let it be in vain."*

If I had let my feet step louder, or opened the door faster—if I had tried to run in that instant, he would have surely seen the locket and brought me to my death. So I slipped out the front door with ease watching the fading bald head of a murderer.

I have thought of nothing more seriously ever since: "How my hatred burns for him!"

I ran past the gas station and in the midst of my run I stopped to think. Every thought was daunting and discouraging and made me feel so vulnerable.

"Where am I going?

... I have one hundred dollars' worth of bills acquired by stealing from Owen... Yes, like Eric, I was a filthy thief. My mother didn't condone larceny... I consider homicide to be a worse evil, however... Oh how I hated that creature!"

I wished in that moment that I could kill him. I wished it with all my heart.

Anyway, the hundred was certainly not enough for a plane ticket, "And before that should enter my mind, what does a plane even look like?" I'd seen drawings of them, but not a real one, or even a photograph.

Quickly, I became distracted by what I believed to be the more important matter at hand. "Who am I to say goodbye to? Eric or Justin?"

This was possibly a petty judgment, and perhaps my priorities weren't in order, but what does that matter?

Those two mattered so much to me.

I also wanted to see Christian again. April and Miranda as well, but I didn't want to spend forever explaining things.

I didn't want to change my mind. I had to leave.

I could only see a problem with going to see Eric. He would do his best, and probably succeed at convincing me to stay, even after I'd tell him the whole story.

He'd say, "Tough it out and stay with us. You can handle it just for the rest of your school time."

I winced at my hypothetical response; "I will be dead before my eighth grade year even enters my hopes."

I would not let my mother die in vain and I was so afraid to die... even though I knew that anything beyond death may be better than the abuse that I knew.

My life was good though. I loved... I still had a family: a family that I created and brought together.

I knew that going to see Justin would help my situation and strength better than anything. He would send me off with a shove no matter how much he wanted to keep me here. He wasn't selfish at all. He'd know what was best and want just that for me. His friend. His ally.

So, I was off to the Diner. Justin's window was cracked open like always. I opened it further and squinted into the darkness. The whites of his eyes glinted in the light of the moon, and it was clear that he was wide awake. As I moved further forward, his whole face came slowly into view. His crooked-toothed smile made my heart ache in spite of my fondness towards it.

"Hi, Joslin. Come for some butt-whopping in Candy Land..."

I knew what he was going to say next, "Or are you too chicken?" or "chicken isn't a candy" or something like that.

Then he saw my duffle bag in hand and my tears that I didn't know were there at first. His eyebrows tilted and he became such a serious little boy, despite his utter cheerfulness a minute before.

Justin helped my other leg over the edge and balanced me as I shifted into the room. His warm, curled pointer fingers gently wiped the tears from my eyes.

I looked him straight in the face and started to slightly stutter some gibberish. Once I realized I needed to wait to talk, I started breathing slowly, counting my breaths.

My eyes never left his as I showed him the locket and told the story of my encounter in the attic. When he closed his eyes to hold back his tears (Because apparently, as I've said before, boys aren't allowed to cry) I looked at his whole face and the wonderful sight that I was abandoning.

That was when I told him that I had to run away... He paused and asked me if I realized that I was eight-years-old. We both laughed in a shaky sort of way, feeling awkward, scared, and sad.

He lifted an index finger and left me for only a moment and returned with a wallet. "There's three hundred dollars in here," He said, "I've been saving it up from kindergarten, doing my chores and such."

*I hesitated. I felt too **needy**.*

Justin glared at me, "Joslin, do you wanna survive er not? Just take the stupid money."

I smiled and took the wallet from him, "Thank you, Justin."

Then he looked down and touched the locket on my neck, "Don't..." I said.

He looked up at me, "I'm only looking at it."

He gently lifted it. To my surprise it lifted easily, despite its strong hold on me.

"It's glowing," he said.

I watched it, "You're right..." that was all I could say for the longest time.

Then, "It glowed when it was on my mother's neck as well. It's really not that great."

He chuckled, looking down.

Then after a pause, he looked up at me, "Be careful out there, Jos." He said as his eyes filled with tears.

And before I could say, "Come on, Justin, I will," He pulled my head into him by my necklace and kissed me once on the lips.

I chuckled, "I love you too, Justin."

And I hugged him.

I think we hugged for about fifteen minutes.

We stayed there, wrapped around each other. Of course I didn't know what he was thinking, but my mind flooded with thoughts and plaguing curiosity. Every time he took a breath, I felt like love itself was holding me (not to be corny or anything).

It was the greatest leap from the lowest to the highest feelings I'd ever felt. At that moment I realized:

I was leaving my only comfort in the world. The one person who loved me enough to let me go and at the same time, promised that he wouldn't.

He was here in my arms and would stay in my thoughts. The funny thing was that now that I could leave, I didn't want to. I felt so connected with him.

I thought, "Perhaps I can just stay with someone...

April's family… Stay here…" … "Owen…"

My thoughts were just blotched. They searched for coherence…

"Goodbye, Joslin."

I nodded, more to myself than to him, confirming that I would flee.

When I broke free from him, we were both crying and I gasped because I didn't realize how sad I was. Our eyes were locked into a staring contest by accident. Then out of embarrassment, we looked away.

Life always has to be so underrated.

I slipped out the window, unable to speak. I tilted my head, slinking through and I was off! I concentrated on leaving once my back was turned. I didn't dare to glance back.

It was like the story of the woman-pillar-of-salt that my mother read to me from the Bible. Looking back would be foolish, so I kept my eyes forward and ran…

My breath quivered.

My legs moved, one, and the next after, pulsing and speeding. My adrenaline raced, and my heart screamed. It was a power run, a freedom call, and the biggest stretch I made from one life to the next.

…I remembered Tip Sod Town as the hardest place to get to… and the hardest place to leave…

I had several hitchhiking stories to tell tourists.

Miraculous tales about how I magically did not get raped, even though the chances were immense.

One family picked me up after I got to a heavy traffic road. I'd never seen so many cars all at once, and even though the white "walk" light was shining and *people stopped accordingly, I was too scared to walk across.*

I kept my thumb up, and eventually found myself doing that same retarded kindergartener thing that I've made fun of:

I waved my hand in ridiculous motions, thumb now swerving in an interesting formation, and the cars continued to pass. I walked down a stretch of the highway that intersected the dead-end one that I'd just emerged from, and continued to wave at people.

The waving tired me out, of course, and I knew it would, but the thought was that perhaps someone would notice me, and then I could rest.

At last, ironically when I'd decided to rest a minute and sit on my duffle, a man peeked out of his passenger side window.

"You need a ride, sweetheart?"

I just looked up at him, weary-eyed. I was still crying, but silently. I mustered up no strength to speak.

A child pressed a button to open the van's sliding door from inside. She was about four years old, and blonde. She had pigtails in and a lollipop in her mouth.

"Thank you for helping..." I said to the woman driving the van.

"It was Howard's idea, sweetie, but you're welcome"

I didn't give a damn whose idea it was. 'Thank you to the both of you then!' I thought. 'You're the one driving, you could have said no...'

"Where do you come from, honey?" Howard asked.

"Lucy, leave her alone please, daddy's asking a

question." said the driver.

Lucy had been offering up her lollipop to me. Over and over again, she shoved it in my face so that it stuck to my lips, and then she peeled it away and gave it a lick.

Lucy ceased the action abruptly upon hearing her mother's voice. Her big orange-brown eyes opened very wide, as if she had a reason to fear her mother. She appeared to be very naïve to me.

I laughed a little, "I am not trying to go back to where I came from."

Howard had a very wavy full head of grey hair. His wife appeared to be much younger than he was. So many lines appeared in his forehead that I found it funny to try and count them.

He leaned over and whispered something to Viola? Violet? Her name was loud in his whisper, but I didn't get it clear enough.

She nodded, "Sweetie pie, we're just trying to help you."

I sighed, "Please, my name is **Joslin**."

"Okay..." she said, "Joslin, dear, we want to make sure you're safe. How old are you?"

"I am eight-years-old. I live in..."

I was trying to think. What were places close to Alabama? Oh, my knowledge of the states was okay, but... Florida! Florida was close on the map, right?

"Florida. I don't know where exactly, I've been staying with my uncle, and he is very abusive."

Viola or whatever... her eyes shifted from looking at mine through the rearview mirror, to Howard and then at Lucy.

"Joslin, you know..." She panicked, "You know we don't talk about grown-ups like that unless we REALLY mean it, right? You know that a spanking isn't abuse, right?"

She was kind of annoying me. She looked at her own daughter the whole time she was talking, trying to teach her a lesson or something, and her eyes were growing wider and wider the longer I waited to respond.

I said nothing. All I did was remove my collared shirt. I had just a tank underneath, exposing my wounds and my scars.

My neck had healed, but the marks were still there. They were patches of discoloration, and indents of scars that would most likely be there forever.

Our driver couldn't take her eyes off of my neck.

"Violet!"

Howard shouted at her.

Rightfully so. We came slightly over the dotted line, and at even just 70 miles an hour, that wasn't acceptable.

So, I knew her name finally. 'Too bad,' I thought, 'I liked Viola better'.

Then I laughed to myself a little.

"Joslin" Violet gulped. "Do you know your uncle's name?"

I hesitated. This wasn't a difficult question and there was no good reason for me not to tell her. Still, in a moment of stupidity and foul logic, I told her 'no'.

"Tsk," went her tongue between her teeth.

This woman was too good natured, I felt, because as an attribute to her goodness, she worried too much.

I wanted to say, "He doesn't matter now! I am free!" and smile so big, grin so wide.

"Okay, girls, we're going to stop here at this gas station. Joslin, will you please put your duffle bag in the back?" Violet said.

I obliged.

"Thank you. We won't be long."

We were just off of interstate 65, and I heard them say they were headed toward Albany. I personally didn't know where Albany was, and I was very afraid that we'd still be in Alabama, which—to me—meant that we'd be too close.

I didn't want to go extremely far, but I didn't want to be super close either.

Before long, I became anxious. They'd been in there far too long, and although daybreak hadn't set in completely, I was more afraid of their destination than I was of the dark.

Besides that, most of the darkness had subsided and I'd be able to see clearer in just a while.

I placed two twenty dollar bills on the seat beneath me, and I turned to Lucy.

"Tell your parents, 'thanks' for me, okay, kid?"

Lucy nodded, and asked me, "Where are you gonna go?"

"Some place far away." I smiled. "Where I can be hidden and free at the same time!"

Lucy looked at me with so much wonder in her eyes. My mother's locket was beaming a bright pink, and it reminded me so much of Aina.

So, Lucy, in turn, held fond memories for me, and

every time I think of her tiny freckled face, I think of my mother being happy.

When the locket glowed, Lucy laughed and kept her eyes on it until I reached for my duffle and left the van. "Thank you, Lucy. Have a good life." I said, smiling.

I didn't feel sad at all in that moment. I meant those last words I said to her with all of my heart, and they warmed my spirit even more than before.

I crept around the green glow of the gas station, sure that they'd look out the window at any time, but confident that the darkness covered me well enough.

I ran into a cluster of trees nearby: following the road would just allow them to catch up with me. I ran too fast to know how Violet and Howard reacted to my absence.

After however long I'd been trudging through the trees bushes and leaves, my stomach rumbled very loudly.

I glared at it, "Hush." I said, "I can't eat right now, and I know this. I need to find my way out of the forest here first."

It wasn't really a forest. I popped out of there several times, running into people's backyards.

In about ten minutes, I think I walked a big semi-circle onto a street called "Hemley Avenue" and I was so hungry and tired that I became dizzy, and I had to rest on the curb.

I don't know how long I walked, but I knew it had been a day since I ate last.

"Hey."

It was a woman's voice that tried to wake me.

"You dead, kid?" She said, "Hey, hey..."

She repeated the word "hey" about fifteen times, and I was so irritated that I yelled at her.

"What?" I said, glaring angrily.

"Have a sandwich, kid."

It was a beautiful sandwich. It had three meats in it, roast beef, turkey, and chicken, some lettuce, cheddar cheese, and French bread.

I grabbed it from her and ate.

"Eat slowly, or you'll barf it up later, and I'm not cleaning it."

"Thank you." I said, muffled, my mouth full of delicious juices and crumpled bread. Some crumbs spilled out, and I refused to talk anymore until I was finished eating, not wanting to waste an ounce of the food.

"Alright..." she said, while I was chewing that last wonderful bite, I'd popped the small last bit into my mouth, and closed it giddily. "So, my name's Ava Jo, and you are?"

"Joslin Olive." I said,

Weird.

Nobody had ever told me their middle name before, so I never told mine. I felt like it wasn't even a part of my name, and I was lying, but my memories of spelling out my name when I was smaller corrected my doubt.

"Hah. Cool. Mind if I call ya Jo?" She said.

I guessed that she was excited about my initials. I felt excited because I was ready to tell her "yeah, I do mind, it's Joslin..."

Yet, she was a fun, and sweet woman, and I finally looked at her face.

She was smiling very wide. She had one golden

tooth and one that was completely missing. Her hair was long, blonde, and curly, and she had real dandelions laced into it in a semi-neat fashion.

"Oh, what the heck," I said, smiling back at her.

She'd been so kind to me, that I should not have minded her poking at my pet peeves. Also, it wasn't as though I'd know her for an incredibly long time, I was planning to live in Florida and she didn't appear to live there.

"Well, before you set down to rot in the sun, Ol' Ava Jo saw you walking. Seemed to me that you were a lady on a mission!" she said.

"Well, yeah, I suppose it's kind of a mission. Is running away from an abusive man considered mission material?"

I waited for the common response: That horrified, "what-the-hell?" look did **not** appear on her face.

Ava Jo just hollered fast and loudly, "Well, sure thing, it does. You're defiant! You're fighting the man that beat ya down! Question is, do ya have a plan?"

I couldn't help myself, "What the hell?"

Ava Jo laughed a smidgen, but it was mostly inaudible, and very airy, as if she were trying about to hack up a lung.

"I'm sorry ma'am, for my impoliteness, and it's not that I don't agree with you, it's just that your reaction..."

"You're a smart lady, Jo. Come walk with me for a moment."

Ava Jo was still smiling, but not quite as wide, and her tone changed from a chaotic-playful into a happy-sincere one. I appreciated it.

I walked with her across "Hemley Avenue", and she talked to me, "Have you ever heard the phrase, 'misery loves its company'?"

I nodded.

Truthfully, I didn't remember ever hearing the phrase, but I was sure I'd be enlightened, and I understood the meaning mostly.

"It's one of those truths of this world that humans can't escape.

"People have put the phrase itself into disarray, and my belief is that it carries two prominent meanings today: One is that a person in misery loves having people around. The second is the original meaning: 'I'm in agony, I want you to be as well'."

I nodded, and waited for her to continue.

"I'm old, Jo. I've known plenty of people who have been beaten (most of them women), and some killed. They were strong people, those who survived and even those who didn't. Everyone has their own story, and they're ready to tell it, or show it to whoever when the time comes.

By running away, not only are you resisting this man, but you're making your story more interesting. How can I react badly to this? This is a good thing. You see what I'm saying?"

A lot of her ideas didn't seem to tie in together, but I liked every word that she said and the sentiment attached.

I nodded, and smiled, "Thank you!" I said, and I grinned, "Thanks for the sandwich, too."

I walked across the street (back to my duffle that sat on the curb) and gripped the handle, and started walking down Hemley.

Ava Jo said, "Hey!" once again.

I laughed, "Yes, Ms. Ava Jo?"

"Well don't you want a ride, crazy?"

Ms. Ava Jo's appearance was humble and ragged. She looked like a person that a lot of people would call filthy and most wouldn't trust.

She'd won me over with her little speech though, and we climbed into her concoction of a van together.

It was a very miraculous piece of artwork, actually, contrived from scrap and junk metal that had been welded together.

I didn't like the way it looked, but the history behind every little detail amazed me, and of course, Ava Jo yammered on, explaining everything.

We started driving along Interstate 65, and she was in and out of random stories. And that was when I asked her about the van itself.

"Well, it's a hippie!" she exclaimed.

I paused.

"'Course I guess there's some things you're still too young to know," she said, laughing and coughing, "Heck, **I'm** too young to know.

"Well. Eh, hippie vans were created in... I think... the 1960's. I'm sort of a vintage lady," she said, fanning herself with her hand.

"Well, you could say that!" I laughed.

This woman was essentially telling me that she's kept parts of this car preserved for almost 200 years.

"Alright, well, anyways, more on that later. Where to, mon cap-i-tain?"

"Well," I said, "I was thinking perhaps Florida. On a nice white sandy beach. I've heard that it's lovely, and the weather is fine."

"If you consider raining 'fine' sure."

"... It can't be sunny all the time..." I said, smiling wistfully.

"Too true." She said, grinning, "Onward to Florida!"

■■■

Joslin presently plops herself on the floor in her designated room in Miranda's house.

They'd just finished going "out on the town" and Joslin was really excited and nervous when they left the house.

They walked up the hill past the mansion field and got into her Bugatti. Joslin guessed that Miranda just didn't feel like walking, or perhaps was still looking for opportunities to show off her car that looked to be about as new as it gets (even with the Alabama dust all over it).

However, Miranda didn't stop the car at the Diner or the Bar or anywhere in the town.

Joslin was slightly disappointed, but also partially relieved knowing she had more time to spare before seeing her old allies.

"Miranda, where are we going?"

"I told'ya, sweet pea, out on the town. We're gonna get some color in that skin and some life in that step!"

By color, Joslin assumes she means "sun". Joslin doesn't hate the sun, but she never felt the need to "get some sun".

Her parents always remained warm without the sun. Sure, they weren't even close to tanned, and perhaps Miranda also would've thought that they "needed color" if she ever had the chance to meet them. To Joslin, however, they were perfect.

Anyway, Miranda's not actually talking about the sun. Miranda wants her to wear make-up.

They walk into a small salon in the city (about a two hour drive during which Miranda plays extremely loud rap music) and they sit down to wait.

"Miranda, why did you bring me here? I hate make-up."

"Well, maybe you'll acquire a liking towards it. You never know."

"No... naw, come on, Miranda, let me go... You know what, let's go somewhere else! Let's go to a playground!"

"What are you, five?"

"No, but I hate make-up"

Despite Joslin's pleas to *not* go, and her disapproval in the chair, and her grunts while glaring at the mirror, Miranda seemed very satisfied when their day out was over.

During the drive home, she said, "I don't know what's wrong with you. You were all cooped up in that house. I was setting the bird free. L. O. L."

L. O. L.

That abbreviation used to be for "laughing out loud". It had been transformed into the very retro-hip phrase that just filled in space and annoyed Joslin. Miranda used it right there as a buffer for any awkwardness that may have occurred.

"Miranda... I'm not into make-up, for one..."

Joslin just sighed after her attempt of complaining. The issue with Joslin's and Miranda's relationship right now is that Joslin sees her companion as nothing but a prissy little girly-girl and she has a very human dislike for that trait.

It isn't as though Joslin's not girly too, but she 'sure as heck never was prissy'. Miranda's also very... vain and materialistic in Joslin's perspective.

Joslin had a tad bit of narcissism while she was little, but her excuse was having been her parent's world, and even after they died—that was how she saw herself.

*She **was** the world.* Well, the most important thing in the world to the two people most important to her. With that knowledge, she held and still holds herself in the highest regard.

They drove through Tip Sod Town again, past the old neighborhood, then the lot, the Diner, and the old school, and into the new lot beside the mansion field.

Joslin kept looking at her dolled-up face in the rearview mirror, pulling at her cheeks and messing with her eyelashes, even with the Bugatti parked.

"Oh, would you stop that?" Miranda shouted, "You look gorgeous! The foundation isn't too dark (which was a huge accomplishment, by the way), and the eye shadow makes your eyes pop!"

Joslin grunted once again, as she got out of the car and closed the door.

The rest of the night was uneventful, and since, in Joslin's eyes, it seems that all she'd done that day was run an errand, she's still stir-crazy, bored, and unhappy in the labyrinth house.

The structure has so many secret doorways, which were super entertaining for the first month she'd been there, but Joslin had been used to actually *talking* to people in Florida. She needed to *break free* and talk to someone who wasn't so vain.

2145

"Aren't you gonna stay with me? Look after me, Ava?" I said.

It surprised the eight-year-old me that I had tears welling up in my eyes. I swallowed, and the tears ceased to push forward...

Earlier that day, we traveled.

■■

Ava Jo liked to take the path less traveled to get to places. I remember the weird gravel roads and rural chains we took instead of the interstate.

And if ever she did feel the need to get onto the highway, she'd shout beforehand, "I'VE GOT A NEEEEED FOR SPEEEEEEEEEEEEEEEED! WOO HOO!"

Immediately, in those moments, I'd sit in an actual chair in the van and buckle up.

The funny thing is that her van only comfortably went 60 miles per hour.

When the speed limit was 70, and you had everyone around you going 40 miles over the limit, this became an issue.

Thankfully, while we were traveling, most drivers paid close attention to our odd little vessel, and nobody crashed into us.

Interestingly enough, Ava Jo seemed to disregard all life anyway.

The truth of the matter was that she truly didn't care whether or not she lived or died. She was a free spirit, "as free as a bird".

*She didn't **want** to endanger herself, but she didn't care if it happened. She took life by stride.*

*We managed, however, to get to Florida in one piece. Ava Jo was about to just drop me off and head on off to nowhere land again. (Wherever she wanted to go was where she'd head to, but she didn't even **know** what she wanted most of the time.)*

"Aren't you gonna stay with me? Look after me,

217

Ava?" I said.

Ava looked at me. Her expression was the same as always—an unreadable, reddened cheerfulness encompassed her, even while she frowned in the piercing heat of the sun.

"You don't need me, kid." She said, grinning, "But I will tell ya what though. I'm gonna give ol' hippie here a break, and we'll hang out for a lil' while."

I smiled back at her. And she helped me gather some things that I needed over the next few days. She taught me how to braid yarn and twine and weeds to make necklaces, and we set up my little shop in a relatively good tourist spot—not too noticeable, but in plain view.

She pitched in and bought me a bed and helped buy all the wood and tin and furnishing to make my house-shop.

She was my most resourceful (and oldest) ally. But she, like everyone else, could not stay a part of my life. She left me when it appeared that my small eight-year-old being could take care of itself.

I kind-of still miss her today. But it's not something that makes me sad, like the thoughts of my parents. There's the hope and the small desire to have her fun come back into my life.

Like the little girl, Lucy, who I also only saw for a few moments, she will always make me smile, but I will probably never see her again. And that's okay.

Anyway, most tourists didn't mind that I wasn't in school as young as I was, and I guessed that at this time, southern states were laid back about just about everything.

Even so, it wasn't like I stopped my education by

any means.

It took the three hundred dollars that Justin gave me to pay for building my "Surf and Shell" shack by the ocean and pay for some food that lasted two days.

After that, the money I made by selling souvenirs on what used to be an empty beach bought my food and eventually some textbooks. I spent nine years living on my own, in that pitiful shack with one room. Sometimes I traveled into town to go to the bathroom, but most of the time I just went in the ocean—hey, it was convenient...

I also traveled into town to eat until I learned how to fish. I didn't really care enough to try and teach myself survival skills and Ava Jo was long gone. She spent a while with me "givin' ol' hippie a rest" and then I spent a little over a year by myself.

Some days when I lived alone, I nearly starved. I hovered around the back exits of restaurants, where they'd throw bags of half-eaten (still good and salvageable) food away.

I'd eat until I discovered something nasty and had to enter a battle with my gag reflex, then, after a while my gag reflex shut off. I could've eaten a raw, dead cat if I wanted to.

This savage behavior lasted for a long while. I can't tell you how long—I just was not myself.

I felt like something mortal and primal took over my spiritual being. The faerie child who thrived off of the blood of curious nature had been trapped by an animalistic human shell. She was vicious and vial.

■■

2146

Once, this creature I became could be seen rummaging in the trash bags behind "Bürgersteig". The disdainful air in the German butchery's trash alley didn't bother me until the day I met Landon Garland.

He found me shoving a potato salad with bits of cinnamon cake into my mouth—at least that was what I thought it was.

Mr. Garland was a 21-year-old man when I met him at age nine. He had hair pulled into dreads in certain areas and just tangled in others. Aside from Christian and the animated Tarzan, he was the only boy I'd ever known with such long hair.

*"Are you eating **garbage**?" Landon asked.*

"Yeah, what's it to you?" I said rudely with my mouth full... I had become sort-of a barbaric human child. I hadn't lost all of my graceful habits, but they were most certainly in a deep hibernation.

By the time Landon found me in the garbage, I was a public barbarian (as destructive as a frail and secretive girl could allow herself to be).

"It's nothing to me, go on and eat that diseased shit if you want."

I frowned at him, and looked down at my potato salad. I suddenly realized it was oozing brown substances and had a piece of gum on the surface near a chunk of cinnamon cake.

My gag reflex kicked in and I vomited sweet sustaining leftovers.

With my throat burning, and empty stomach angrily throwing acids to and fro, I turned toward Landon and scowled.

"What the hell is wrong with you?" I shouted, "I'm a child! What are your intentions?"

I had stood up and pointed my arm straight forward, flexing, looking as threatening as I could... I was ready to start a fight if I had to with this fit young man.

Landon Garland was taken aback.

"What the hell is a lady like you doin' in an alley way?" he asked me.

I looked back at the disgusting food, and the pungent regurgitated food, and sighed, "I don't make enough money to sustain myself. They will not allow me to have a job, and I cannot allow myself to enter an orphanage."

"We've got good Foster care here, little girl, whole neighborhoods for it."

"No." I said, glaring at him.

"Well, kid, I'm not taking care of you, so you should make up your mind. Orphanages, or disease and starvation."

"I won't starve." I replied softly.

"Oh, but you will!" he replied, stepping forward slightly, and leaning his sweaty arm against the brick of the building.

"I can't get a disease." I said somberly.

Landon laughed, "You say that like it's the worst thing ever..."

He didn't know anything about it, but I was beginning to really think as I sat there with my legs buried in the trash. I thought about how terrible it was to still be living and I wondered how I could ever die if I kept healing.

I wondered how Owen had the ability to refrain from killing me and that thought gave me the notion that he must've been incapable.

"Because I'm Joslin O. Tilda, forever doomed to be

immortal." I muttered inaudibly.

I glared at Landon once again, "What am I to you? Why are you butting your nose into my life? Just because of a sick interest in poor little girls, or because you're too retarded to understand that you look like a creeper right now and you think you're just 'being a friend'?"

"Woah, little girl, now tha-hahat's the LAST thing I want! Friends? Pft. With a—what are you— an eight-year-old? You're too young and you talk too old."

"Then leave me alone, idiot." I said, rolling my eyes.

"I'm not gonna let you alone, kid... you'll kill yourself."

He came closer to me.

"Don't you touch me!" I shrieked. With hulking claws, my voice scratched at the edge of my throat near my tongue.

Normally, I'd ultimately trust this stranger and let him help me out; not only because it would relieve me, but also because I was curious.

Like I said, though, I had a barbaric transformation into an animal that wanted only to eat, sleep, and make waste. Landon was trying to get in the way of that.

When he'd told me to go ahead and eat that garbage, my regular thoughts and cares reappeared and I realized I had suppressed my gag reflex for months. I didn't like the realization—I didn't want to think about my fantasy, my curiosity, or myself in general.

My own existence wrapped completely around my parents, and they were dead. There was nothing I could do about it, so why bother with their memories?

Landon, however, started an intervention without either of us realizing it.

My goal at the time was to undo my life essence. I wasn't aware of it yet, but my entire spirit was built upon curiosity, and I just didn't care enough to be curious anymore.

His presence didn't move me, until he essentially forced me to stop eating garbage by calling upon the good forces of vomit. From that point on, I became nervous about almost everything. I didn't know how to act, because I wasn't aware of who I was anymore.

My life was shifting...

■■

2154

In the back of Miranda's car when she was whisking Joslin away, back into Alabama, the windows were rolled up. There were already condensation art pieces on the inner sides of the back doors as well as the window in the very back of the car.

Miranda hated the rain, and Joslin never understood why. This rain today brought her into a rant of thoughts. Rain created closure for her...

The rain had washed her blood away many times in the past. Not only blood, but filth. Physically and mentally, it cleansed her in both joy and pain. It gave her hope that a god or **the** God might be there and he had a plan, like people say he does.

Also, she thought, *there could be many gods, like Miranda believes. Maybe they were all just fighting over*

223

my happiness. Or maybe the gods were too busy to control my life, and when it was left in my hands, it corrupted itself a bit.

Another thought was that God could be an overseer of all of the muses and humans in the world and he just let the whole Earth run wild.

The last thought was the one I stuck with, because I had the most proof for that one... I knew exactly what I was, and my life could certainly be considered wild.
■■

The chaotic comeback from Florida into Alabama happened when she met Miranda, who was taking a little weekend get-away for her own enjoyment. Because that's what rich people do...

Randomly, and completely out of the blue she appeared with her Jamaican-looking braids and bikini, with sort-of-peach freckles on her dark face...

"O my God! O my God! Joslin? I can't believe it's you! Look at you!"

Look at me? What is there to look at? I'm skinnier than a toothpick, as pale as a ghost, and I live in a tin-roofed shack in god-damned Florida.

"Hey... you!" *I admit; I didn't recognize her. The last time I saw her was when I was in third grade and she was in fifth. I can't believe she recognized me.*

"You don't recognize me do you?"

That's the general idea when someone greets you without using your name.

"I'm having a hard time, could you help me?"

"Well, do you remember Tip Sod?"

Joslin hadn't expected that.

The locket on her chest thumped with her own heart.

Here she thought this "chick" was a tourist and then she mentioned the one place that no one even knows exists. (I mean, sometimes the people living there don't even know it exists.) Since Joslin knew her, and she looked like a snobby little rich girl, she guessed right:

"Miranda?"

The princess squealed.

It was a really high-pitched, *"I'm a Barbie girl,"* squeal that would never come out of Joslin's lips.

"O my God," Joslin said, "it's been forever..."

She hadn't even gotten to the middle of her sentence when Miranda ran around to the inside of the shack and hugged her like there was no tomorrow.

"O my god, Joslin. Do you want to go back to Tip Sod with me?"

Before she could say no, Miranda continued, "My step-dad sort of gave my mom and me some money! It's too long of a story, I'll tell you 'bout it if ya want in the car. Right now I'm living in my own little mansion in Tip Sod and I *know* you loved it there,"

You don't know anything, Miranda.

225

"So I was wondering if you wanted to live with me!"

Joslin tried ignoring the fact that "little" and "mansion" didn't go together, but the thought left a big smirk on her face.

She was about to think up a very amazing excuse not to go, but the only one that worked was the truth about Owen. No one could know about that unless they already did (Sort of like the public knowing about how to find the city of Atlantis, or the even more difficult Tip Sod, Alabama).

There were also *more* excuses to actually *go* with her anyway.

#1: If it was a mansion and she's talking about Tip Sod, it's obviously far away from Owen's house. Owen wouldn't allow any big fancy house next to him and his tattered glory.

#2: It's in Tip Sod. I'll get to see Eric and April and Justin after nine years.

#3: I'll get to see Justin. And that one, I list twice for a reason...

The odds were officially against me.

I knew in the back of my mind that people could change and if Justin changed, I could handle it. I mean; I've changed as well.

We all went through puberty and our different life lessons... I'm sure we all had our crazy stories to tell. Still, I was a little sad that I hadn't been a part of their lives for so long, and my curiosity peaked.

Miranda mentioned him once in the car.

"You know Justin?"

I nodded, and she started talking more, but the truth was that I didn't care to hear what she had to say about him. I wanted to see him. I wanted to experience how he changed on my own accord. I was also too busy thinking about all of my past to listen to Miranda's stories anyway.

I cared a lot about Miranda for a little while in third grade, but not enough to accept her weird-pop-culture personality now. She really annoyed me...

We passed the black oak house on the side of the road. Shivers ran up and down my back as my imagination clouded the area with raging fire.

"What shall I do with Owen?

I want to kill him. Perhaps I could ask Miranda to stop the car... light a match..."

Joslin didn't have any matches.

Perhaps it was for the best. Joslin entertained herself with the idea that he was already dead. She would never have to sink to his level... or have the urge.

So she urged her mind to forget (not an easy task). She concerned herself with simply watching the rain. She tapped gently on the locket that pulsed lightly on her neck, and its dim glow of red lit up her eyes quickly turning to pink with her softer thoughts.

She covered it gently with her hands and stole a glance at Miranda. She still rambled on but Joslin couldn't hear her at all, maybe she was just chewing gum or something... She couldn't tell, but Miranda hadn't noticed the locket. That was the important thing.

■■

Anyway, as flashbacks continue while Joslin thinks and thinks to herself, alone in the "little mansion" she becomes bothered.

She may be nervous to see anyone from the past, but Joslin O. Tilda is no coward. She's not even shy like your average outcast. Joslin chatted with all kinds of unusual and average people alike while in Florida.

Barely anything made her shy anymore. She had even practiced dancing in nothing but a bikini on the shore late at night. Her bruises and scars glimmered in the moonlight. They were a light off-white infected with the average pink or black coloration.

Still, she never quite learned how to get into any relationships, and she thinks of herself as a bit immature in the dating area.

Miranda was always out with her boyfriend or just "hitting the town" and Joslin had been invited, but to Hell with that idea! She spent enough time with Miranda and she'd rather keel over and die than to be their third wheel.

So, after Miranda left again, that same night the girls had gone out to get a makeover, Joslin had slipped off into the morning's darkness around 1:30 a.m. in her light grey overcoat.

■■

There's the slim chance that Miranda could hop into view at any moment, finally come home after a night of partying and ask to go out with her, but the thought is mute in Joslin's mind. Miranda never got home before 4a.m.

Voices in Joslin's mind say, "press on, let's explore!" As she finally leaves the house to venture through the night, her legs tingle, as the muscles in her feet taper on.

(Truthfully, they'd been asleep, and the sudden movement stirs the blood, making her feel strange and uneasy, but her curiosity transforms the feeling into "thrill".)

Joslin walks into the forest once again, as she'd done so many times before. Her shoes start to soak through with water from the forest dew, and her socks slosh around and lap at her feet.

Twilight creeps into view, and everything disintegrates softly into a shadowy kingdom for the night.

Joslin walks on.

The wood becomes drier the closer into town she walks. As she removes her socks and shoes, she tries to remember where her old tree house is. Coming from the opposite side of town, it's difficult to navigate to anything recognizable.

Suddenly though, Joslin comes into view of a small clearing, from which houses of the old neighborhood can be seen.

The two rows of five houses are vaguely lit with dim streetlamps, which appear to be less light than that which spilled into the clearing:

A waning—attenuating full moon is plastered to the sky, and it streams its pale light onto an old stone-built fountain. The fountain sits in the middle of a gravel path, which leads into the old neighborhood.

Bushes and small flowers are popping up from random places in the path along with dirt and mud patches. Joslin walks onto the path from the chaotic brush she'd been trudging in, and looks up at the moon.

She sighs, and prepares herself to sit there and sleep for a while. The oversized overcoat she wears warms and comforts her, and covers her petit frame completely as she sits down by the fountain.

She covers her head with the hood and starts to drift to sleep, more comfortable on the stone than in her new "comfy" bed.

"God... why...?"

That voice. A young man's voice starts to pray. The source is so close to her, but she'd heard no footsteps. Joslin meekly peeks from beneath her jacket's hood. The moon must be hidden by some clouds for the time being, because the man is standing so close to her, but it's too dark for her to see his face.

"What the Hell..." he says.
Joslin's heart pounds into her throat. She knows that the man is young, he can't be Owen, and she knows that most

people are harmless in this town, but she is still frightened.

If not frightened, she's at least stirred as the man brushes her hood with his fingertips.

"Todd, you don't know who that is. He's probably sleeping." Another voice said.

"He's prol'y a hobo, huh?" Todd responded, alleviating my hood and giving my heart a break.

"Well, I dunno, it's a really nice jacket, but naw, shouldn't mess with the guy, he's definitely sleeping."

"Ha, ha," the man called Todd laughed as they started to walk away, kicking up stones as they went, "Amp, that's gonna be you in five years..."

"Shut-up, man, my music's doing great." The guy called "Amp" said.

"It's not doing you shit! Where's the money man, eh?" Todd continued to laugh.

I uncovered my head once I heard them walk far enough away.

My black hair started frolicking in the air immediately as the night wind picked up. It whistled stridently, piercing through and around the fabric of my hood. I looked at Justin, walking with his friend back into town. An older, adolescent version of the physically speckled kid that I used to call "ally" walked with a boy I'd never seen before.

I lifted my hand, and started to speak, but the wind made me shiver.

By the time I said, "Justin!" they were too far away to hear me.

As I saw Justin and his new friend walk away, I couldn't contain myself...

--Literally, I could not contain myself.

I wanted so badly to talk to him—to tell him I was there, just say "hi!" or something!

I started walking toward them, briskly, then after a few steps, I abruptly stopped upon an intriguing thought.

"Should I show him what I am?" I breathed the thought aloud through a whispering sigh.

Carefully I searched.

Once the thought came into place, excitement over-took me. My eyes swerved around, hungry for a safe place to put my jacket, night gown and the dear, precious locket. As though carelessly shoved to the side, my mother's locket erupted with life, protesting my absence and expressing my excitement all at once. The light shone so brightly, I feared I'd be seen.

"Shhh!" I said, as I removed my shirt, softly stretching my arms. With the way the world was, I should've felt wrong and overly exposed, I suppose. Yet, I felt so natural and beautiful—naked and bathed in the blanketing dark sensuality of the night.

I breathed one last relaxing human breath, and then turned to the locket lying on the floor. The locket relaxed slightly, but I could still feel its mysterious life calling to me.

However, the curiosity I felt to see Justin's reaction upon meeting me was far greater than any other pull.

"Dim it down!" I whispered with malice force, "Hush. I cannot take your magic with me when we fly. You must hide yourself..."

I allowed myself to speak a final thought to the ever-animated locket. Then, the tharpels detached, and we swarmed into the night.

As a human, I thought about how embarrassed I would be to be naked in front of Justin.

As faeries, my care went away and the thought was invigorating merely for curiosity's sake. I had no way of telling what would happen.

▪▪▪

2147

I found out soon enough—in my years of self-sentenced exile... I discovered that I wasn't fully human.

The knowledge came to me in a dream. (If that's too cliché, so be it, that's how it happened.)

Months ago, after experiencing a full-on human survival mode, Landon took me in... sort of. He didn't truly have the resources to take me in, but he had some helpful knowledge and a convenient soft-spot for me.

I noticed over time that Landon Garland didn't care for children. I guess since I was acting like an animal when we met and an adult when we became more acquainted, I didn't really count at all. We acted like relatives. I didn't see him as a father figure, so I assumed he was a brother (like I'd wanted Christian to be).

Landon taught me how to fish.

Once I trusted him enough (which took only a short amount of time out of necessity because I was very hungry) he took me for a ride across the Panama bridge in his old, beat-up car from 2110. We'd set out on the nice and beautiful, hot, sandy, white beaches near a designated fishing spot.

*Landon lived in the back of a hotel near the beach in the janitor's suite. He said he **was** a janitor, but I never saw the hotel or him in his uniform. He also seemed to have a very relaxed schedule for a janitor, because we would spend days on end catching, and selling, and eating fish.*

For weeks on end sometimes we'd be seen together. One woman called me his daughter once, and most people thought we were siblings. Then, one night, Landon left.

This happened every-so-often.

I figured it must've been during the weekends (although I had no concept of time) and those days must've been the only days he was scheduled to work at the hotel.

Yet since that night, Landon never returned. And on that very night, I had this dream:

It started as if it were that same small reoccurring dream I've had many times over.

The maggot looking creatures appeared to me, small and harmless. They shone bright and were interrelated to me and to each other. This time started out like any other time I dreamed of them, but extended beyond what I'd seen before.

As if I were looking through the scope of a camera's lens, I zoomed out of focus, and I could see my own brain.

Unlike what I'd been taught, my human brain glowed. This glow mocked the glow of my healing wounds and scars and these maggot-like faerie beings. I zoomed out further, and saw my own two eyes.

I woke up with a start on the beach near my shack.

"Tharpels" I stated...

My father coined their name. From what? Neither they nor I know, but we don't and didn't care either—that's not important.

*What **is** important is that the tharpels revealed themselves to me, and I finally knew all that I was capable of doing.*

I sat down on the rocky sands of my beach, and peered into the sun. Their collective voice was peacefully soft, but eerie. It had billions of different tones, undertones and flavors all morphed into one sound, moving about my head.

In unison they whispered, "Joslin...

"We are you... we are your secret..."

I laughed in disbelief as every question I had about myself and my past and my parents disappeared. So many questions I had and in an instant they were eradicated. Within my body, within my skin, the answers sat. Suddenly, I was omniscient to everything involving my life— I knew more information than my human brain could handle.

I realized that pockets of my own memories had to be forever stored within my very core. The tharpels showed me through my own suppressed memories that they were respecting the wishes of my mother, who wanted me to be able to interact normally with humans.

My father agreed that it would be best for me to understand humanity more than "fairyism" as I started out my life. Then eventually, Talib wanted to teach me about Husrodolg: the land that I hailed from.

Talib told me stories, and I suspected nothing but deceit from his mouth, but ever since my self-discovery I slowly saw faerie tales prove their truth.

*I can **see** things now (as Joslin, and as the tharpels) that average humans cannot see.*

For instance? The "grass dragons" from my father's old stories? They're real!

In fact, I come across them all the time! They are beautiful lizard-like creatures that breathe dew onto the grass every morning.

In daytime, usually, that's when one part of their body can be seen: Dragonflies are the hearts of grass dragons. So, as I'm sure anyone could imagine, the beasts come in many different shapes and sizes.

Their scales are transparent, even to me. I can see through them, but I can see their form, the shadow of their scales, their mouths, and their mischievous crocodile's smile.

*Also, as if discovering new creatures wasn't amazing enough, I can actually **control** myself now. Before, without my own conscious consent, I'd split myself into pieces and wander through the night.*

It happened when I was in Owen's prison.

237

Long ago, while I slept, when Owen had the locket trapped away in his attic, we searched for it; for my sake and theirs... for ours?

It's all so funny-sounding to humans, but we are all "the same entity": we are half-human or I am half-tharpel—it doesn't really matter how we put it.

Separated we are invisible, and as a whole, I am Joslin O. Tilda.

Things changed a lot after they told me about their existence when I was ten:

Since then, I've been mostly happier because I can better control things. I send thoughts and memories that I don't need into individual tharpel cells along my body (I call them "tharpel cells" when they're a part of my human form.) I can also control who I allow to see me heal.

I am permitted to know of my own memories. Each time we separate into tharpels, as Joslin I can remember the experience of flying, and being invisible and being **many.**

If I want to know something about the tharpels, my parents, or my own past: my nervous system (which is built upon "tharpel cells") can find the memories and give them to me.

Yet, even though we are all thriving for the same cause (to have a happy life) the tharpels and I tend to need to compromise. This isn't usually necessary since we are "one", but we sometimes need to keep each other in check.

It's similar to muscle memory against logic. Like, say a factory worker does the same thing with a conveyor belt day in and day out. Well, a screw comes loose and some equipment is about to fall on him. Does he continue to do what he's always done? No! He gets the Hell out of there.

Whatever my tharpel cells want is what is natural for me to want, but they can't always tell what's best, which is why they built a human-like brain for my human-like logic to settle down in.

Now... I can't die, because tharpels are immortal, but we try to make it so we're happy in this immortal life. We try to keep away from pain...

They yielded my healing process around Owen so that he wouldn't see the glow and have more reason to experiment with wounding me.

Since they did not glow to heal during those times, some skin tharpel cells became scar tharpel cells.

They have branded themselves with the discoloration forever. "We will always remember..." They seemed to say.

2154

Memories are beautiful even when they are sour, because they are remnants of moments; proof of time. However, presently, my life doesn't involve much *pain like it did before. It burns with the passion of ambitious discovery.*

As I was saying about my transformation: I truthfully could not contain myself.

Justin meant the world to me, and we knew it. My precious items were strewn upon branches within a bush among the copses near the clearing.

I was very nude in the white light. The moonlight seemed to mimic the glow that protruded from my body. Then, as we broke from each other, cell by cell, our faerie bodies stretched and slipped and flickered.

We couldn't see the relation between us and the moon any longer. It was a human comparison. Color didn't exist as we flew. We recognized the moon's presence as beautiful, but also cold and inanimate.

Our lights were breathing and buzzing. We traveled like light and our light traveled like sound, trailing behind us. We had a pulse, and life surrounding had a flavor and extravagance about it.

If Joslin hadn't been so intent on seeing the Justin, we would have explored the night and its mysteries much longer.

We were an elegant flock... or rather a swarm since we were so small. All of us, as we thought of our past as the Joslin, were excited and ever-curious, eager to see the town itself once again.

We peered below into the soft fog of low-rise clouds. Once we flew as far as the Diner, we saw the Justin and the one called "Todd" part ways as the Justin strolled into the front doors of the Diner.

We flew downward.

As Joslin, I remembered that I broke into the back window most of the time in my younger years. So we flew through the window's glass and into Justin's room. Gathering creatures that were invisible, practically stitching my every membrane back together in a matter of seconds, my glow lit up his pitch black room. The glimmer faded just as Justin walked in.

I shivered slightly, mostly because at the age of seventeen, I'd never been naked in front of anyone. I liked the natural feel of nudity, truthfully, but that sounds weird to most humans.

The moonlight flowed through his window in a stream, interrupted with sporadic shadow dams.

Justin plopped onto his twin bed, which squeaked. Upon his landing, a yawn ended in an eruptive sigh.

I hesitated. My body swayed shortly, my mind confused on whether or not to share this secret.

As I looked around his room I was reminded once again that my allies, and I—we had all changed. With that knowledge reconciled, a new notion had risen.

"What if I can't trust him?" I thought.

The tharpels weren't wary. They didn't seem threatened, but for some reason, I was unsure. I suddenly felt for the first time in years that I was somewhere that I didn't want to be.

So, I sat, feet supporting my haunches in a bit of a squat, and I pondered my next action carefully.

There was a blanket on the floor.

So I tried to reach it...

Unintentionally, my breast peeked into the moonlight.

I hadn't noticed until Justin said, "What the crap?"

"Op!" I squeaked, and I ducked back into the dark.

"Okay..." Justin said as he slowly got up.

My heart was pounding, and I just knew that my face had flushed into a soft pinkish red with my embarrassment as he said, "That was nice... Now where's the rest of you?"

He chuckled. Then as I hesitated, he laughed nervously, and I sank lower and lower into the dark corner of the room.

"Maybe this wasn't the best idea..." I thought.

*Then, out of nowhere, my curiosity had a stupid question, "Hey Joslin!" It seemed to say, "I wonder. What would happen if you did **this?"***

So, out of the darkness, I jumped, coming in eye-to-eye with him, my naked body bathed in the moonlight stream and goofy grin lighting up my face:

"Hey, Justin..." I said.

■■■

And as faeries, with curiosity's glow, a light not different from the light of moon, I'll fly.

As us, as me, whatever I am, my story continues. My parents live, and live time and time again. Through me, they thrive.

I'm lucky enough to have known them long before I was born.

My parents are living. My father—through my spells and wizardry, my mother—through my dance and memories.

And as for me? I'll live on through my own curiosity. That's just the way we're built isn't it?

Us tharpels... Us humans?

■■■

www.ingramcontent.com/pod-product-compliance
Lightning Source LLC
Chambersburg PA
CBHW022202170626
46807CB00005B/2321